NO ENTRY ALLOWED

A sign hung on the iron gate at the beginning of the front walk. It read *Betreten Verboten*.

"What's it mean?" Joe asked.

"It says come on in and make yourselves at home. Fridge is full," Frank said.

"Yeah, right."

"Come on. Let's see what we can find before we formally introduce ourselves." Frank scaled the gate and dropped down on the other side. He motioned for Joe to follow him as he approached the front door. It was decorated with a heavy cast-iron knocker shaped like a gargoyle.

Joe peered through the square window cut high in the door. "It's too dark," he said. "I can't see anything."

Frank heard a squeaking sound and looked up—too late. He was yanked off his feet and felt himself rocket into the air.

Books in THE HARDY BOYS CASEFILES™ Series

Available from ARCHWAY Paperbacks

THE HARDY BOYS

CASEFILES™

NO. 119

THE EMPEROR'S SHIELD

FRANKLIN W. DIXON

AN ARCHWAY PAPERBACK
Published by POCKET BOOKS
New York London Toronto Sydney Tokyo Singapore

AN ARCHWAY PAPERBACK *Original*

An Archway Paperback published by
POCKET BOOKS, a division of Simon & Schuster Inc.
1230 Avenue of the Americas, New York, NY 10020

Copyright © 1997 by Simon & Schuster Inc.
Produced by Mega-Books of New York, Inc.

ISBN: 0-671-56119-7

First Archway Paperback printing January 1997

10 9 8 7 6 5 4 3 2 1

THE HARDY BOYS, AN ARCHWAY PAPERBACK and colophon are registered trademarks of Simon & Schuster Inc.

THE HARDY BOYS CASEFILES is a trademark of Simon & Schuster Inc.

Cover photograph from "The Hardy Boys" Series © 1995 Nelvana Limited/Marathon Productions S.A. All rights reserved.

Logo design TM & © 1995 by Nelvana Limited. All rights reserved.

Printed in the U.S.A.

IL 6+

THE EMPEROR'S SHIELD

Chapter

1

FRANK HARDY WEARILY PUSHED his passport under the glass partition. A German customs agent snatched it out of the tray. Although Frank knew the physical description in the document matched him perfectly—six-foot-one, brown hair and eyes, eighteen years old—he was so exhausted that he felt the photo could have been of someone else.

The agent's eyes bored into Frank. "What brings you to Stuttgart, business or pleasure?" he asked in stilted English.

Despite the fatigue of an eight-hour flight, Frank managed a smile. "Both, I guess. I'm here to help with an archaeological survey."

The man's brow wrinkled. "You are an archaeologist?" he said skeptically. Frank knew he should have kept his mouth shut, but it was too late. He reached into the side pocket of the slim, black case that held his notebook computer and pulled out a folder. "Here's the paperwork," he said. "We're here to help an American scientist, Dr. John Maxwell, search for a lost Roman fort near Köbingen."

The guard paged through the papers slowly. "And what is your association with this archaeologist, Dr. Maxwell?" he asked without looking up.

"Friend of the family," Frank replied. Actually, Dr. Maxwell had been his father's roommate in college. He had recently been applying his new underground prospecting techniques in the field and had invited the Hardys to come to Germany during their winter break to help with his research.

The customs agent held up one of the papers. "You hope to discover the jeweled shield of Emperor Decius?"

"That's only a legend," Frank said, shrugging. "Who knows what we'll find."

"You do know that smuggling artifacts out of Germany is strictly forbidden?"

Frank nodded.

"Punishable by fine and imprisonment."

"Yes, I know," Frank said, being careful not to lose his patience.

The official inked a wood-handled stamp and

smacked it on the last page of the passport. *"Danke,"* he said, passing it back to Frank.

"Bitte," Frank replied. He turned down a hall that opened up into the airport's main lobby. The area was crowded with travelers wearing heavy overcoats and parkas. Frank ducked as he walked past a young woman carrying a pair of cross-country skis over her shoulder. It seemed everyone was trying to get somewhere for the New Year celebration that evening.

"Frank, over here!" Frank spotted his girlfriend, Callie Shaw, waving to him from a rental car desk. His younger brother, Joe, stood next to her, filling out forms.

Joe looked up as Frank came over. "Took you long enough," he said. Seventeen-year-old Joe, who had somehow managed to sleep through the trans-Atlantic flight, was raring to go. Six feet tall and blond, Joe always seemed to be in a rush to get to his destination.

Frank dropped his duffel bag and massaged the back of his neck. "The customs guy gave me the third degree about smuggling antiquities."

"Smuggling antiquities?" Callie said. "We'll be lucky if we find any." Pulling her thick, blond hair back into a ponytail, she let it fall down her back.

Frank nodded toward the papers Joe was filling out. "What's this?"

"I'm renting us a car," Joe replied. "A ticket agent was waiting for us out here with a message from Dr. Maxwell. Something about being out in the field all day." Joe handed the papers to the rental clerk and received a set of car keys in return. "I'm driving," he said as the three of them headed to the parking lot.

Outside, Joe stopped at a long row of gleaming German sports cars. He looked at the tag on the keys, and his eyebrows shot up. "Whoa. Check it out. This is ours," he said.

"You're kidding, right?" Frank dropped his duffel bag to the pavement.

"Nope," Joe said, putting on his sunglasses and unlocking the driver's door. "One fire engine red Porsche 911 Turbo. The fastest production car in the world. Especially with me behind the wheel."

"Where do we put our bags?" Callie asked.

"With four hundred horses behind us, who cares?" Joe popped open the hood, and they squished their luggage in as well as they could. Frank's laptop computer and Joe's hiking boots had to go in the tiny backseat with Callie.

The inside of the car smelled of expensive leather. Joe turned the key, and the Porsche roared to life, the flat-six engine racing at first, then settling to a raucous idle. The car rumbled like a rocket about to blast off. Joe threw it into gear and popped the clutch. Without even meaning to, he smoked the tires as they shot out of the parking lot.

"Easy, Mario," Callie teased. She had to sit

sideways in back, her legs stretched out on the seat.

Frank had studied German for two years at Bayport High School, and he used what he'd learned to read the signs directing them to the autobahn. Joe merged into the right lane and cruised there for a few minutes, gauging the speed of the traffic.

"We're going one hundred and ten kilometers an hour in the slow lane," Frank noted.

"That's almost seventy," Callie said. "Better take it easy, Joe."

Joe reluctantly obliged, slowing down enough to take in the view. The superhighway curved through the snow-covered Zugspitze Mountains and along the Neckar River. Signs of civilization dwindled, and across the river, to their left, the Black Forest rose up, a dense strand of blue spruce and other evergreens.

Frank looked at the map Joe had gotten from the rental agent. "It's going to take us over an hour to get to Köbingen."

"Not if I can help it." Joe accelerated and eased the Porsche into the center lane. The turbo engine wailed like a jet turbine behind them.

"So, Frank,' Callie said, "you're the archaeology buff. Fill me in on what's so special about Dr. Maxwell's research."

"I thought you read the file on the plane," Frank said over his shoulder.

"No, Joe had it the whole time. I think he used it for a pillow."

"Hey, I read all of it," Joe said as he checked the mirror and drifted over to the left lane.

"Well," Frank said. "According to the notes Dr. Maxwell sent, his big break came about twelve weeks ago. He was studying some declassified military satellite photos when he noticed a straight line cutting across Köbingen. It turned out to be the remains of a road the Romans built over two thousand years ago."

"He just looked at the photos and saw a road?" Callie asked.

Frank shook his head. "The road is buried ten to twelve feet below the surface. But the photographs were taken with infrared film. The earth is cooler where there's stone underneath, and the tiny differences in temperature show up on the film."

Joe eased off the accelerator as traffic slowed for cars merging on from a ramp up ahead.

"Dr. Maxwell uses computers to enhance the satellite images," Frank continued. "That's how the road showed up."

"That sounds totally cutting edge," Callie said. "Too bad Vanessa couldn't be here."

"I told her we'd E-mail her with all the details," Joe said, thinking about his girlfriend, Vanessa Bender.

"Anyway," Frank continued, "the road itself isn't that important. The point is that a fort was built on the road, at least according to Roman records. We also know that the Neckar River was the border of the Roman Empire when the fort was built."

"I see," Callie said. "Locating the river and the road definitely narrows down the possibilities."

Frank looked out the window just in time to see a huge tractor-trailer rig cut across all three lanes up ahead. Brake lights flashed, and the cars around the truck darted away like a school of fish from a shark. "Watch out for this guy," Frank said.

Joe braked and downshifted, muttering, "Man, he's driving like a mad dog."

The truck driver finally seemed to decide to stay in the center lane. Joe came up on his left and saw on the side of the stark black trailer a picture of a crane. Underneath was written "Zimmermann Construction," in German.

"He's speeding up," Joe said. He set his jaw and downshifted to second, preparing to tear past the truck. But as the Porsche pulled up to the cab, the giant rig swerved toward their lane.

"Watch it!" Frank said. The double rear axles of the cab drew even with the Porsche. Blasts from the truck's airhorn ripped through the car—short, then long.

Joe gripped the wheel and crushed the accelerator, swinging the sports car ahead of the rig. Looking in the rearview mirror, he saw the driver flash his lights angrily.

7

Callie glanced out the back window. "What's this guy's problem?"

"I don't know," Joe said. "All I know is that he's got the size and we've got the speed." He worked the Porsche up through the gears, and watched as the truck receded in the mirror. The sound of the airhorn faded out under the rumble of the 911's engine.

"That was probably just a random crazy driver," Frank said, shifting in his seat to get comfortable. "The Köbingen exit should come up soon."

When the signs for Köbingen appeared, Joe slowed and moved over to the right lane. The Köbingen exit funneled them off the busy super-highway to a narrow lane that led up a steep mountain. The road seemed barely wide enough for the flared fenders of the Porsche.

"Are we going to the top of this mountain?" Callie asked.

"Looks like it," Frank replied.

They wound around one hairpin turn and switchback after another, climbing the whole time. The Neckar River cut through the valley below them like a snake through tall grass.

"We're looking for an iron gate," Frank said. "This could be it up here."

As they approached a drive up on the right, a gate at least fifteen feet tall started to open out toward the road. Joe slowed and was about to pull in when he saw a car come careening down the drive, its tires sending out sprays of ice and gravel.

Joe pumped the brakes hard to keep from skidding, but the other driver lost control trying to avoid the Porsche while still making the turn onto the road. The teenagers could only watch as the car spun across the road toward the cliff.

Joe winced at the sickening crunch that followed. When the sound had passed, he made himself look. The small gray hatchback had slid into a tree, passenger side first.

"Wow!" Frank exclaimed. "A few more feet on either side and it would've gone over."

The Hardys were out of the Porsche in a flash. Joe got to the hatchback and yanked the door open. "Are you okay?"

A girl sat in the driver's seat muttering to herself. She had blue spiked hair and wore black lipstick and about ten different earrings on each ear.

Joe shrugged. "I don't speak German."

The girl kept muttering as she hoisted herself out of the driver's seat and slammed the door violently. She jabbed her index finger into Joe's chest, jangling her bracelets. "Idiot, idiot, idiot!" she shouted, punctuating each word with a jab of her finger. "Did you not see me coming?"

"Ah, now I understand you," Joe said.

Out of the corner of his eye, Joe saw Frank gesturing to him from the other side of the road.

"You guys are in the middle of the street," Frank said. "I think I hear a car coming."

Ignoring Frank's warning, the young woman continued her tirade, stamping her feet and yelling louder and louder. Joe put his hand on the girl's shoulder to calm her down. She knocked his hand away.

The high whine of a diesel engine echoed up toward them. Joe whirled around, but could see nothing where the road leading down the mountain curved away. He turned back to the girl and then saw her eyes go wide.

"Joe," Frank shouted, "get off the road! It's the truck that tried to hit us on the autobahn!"

Chapter

2

JOE SPUN AROUND turned to see the black truck grinding up the hill toward them. It picked up speed as the road flattened out on the approach to the gate entrance.

"Come on," Joe said to the girl. The back end of her car stuck out onto the narrow roadway. He could picture the truck hitting the hatchback and the gas tank exploding. "Let's go," he urged. "We've got to get clear of your car."

"Nein!" The girl pushed up the sleeves of her black leather jacket and stepped to the center of the road.

Joe heard the driver of the truck shifting up through the ten forward gears. The rig's tinted windows hid the driver, but there was no mistaking his intention; the truck was headed straight toward Joe and the others. The wail of the airhorn was so loud, it seemed to make the air around Joe's ears freeze and crack.

The girl had one fist on her hip and shook the other in the air, gesturing defiantly and screaming in German at the invisible driver. Joe didn't know who was crazier, the girl or the driver, but he had no time to figure it out. Squaring his powerful, running back's body toward the girl, Joe went in low and lifted her over his shoulder. As he dashed toward Frank and Callie, he heard the horn again, then felt the gust of air and exhaust against his back as the truck thundered past.

The Hardys and Callie watched wordlessly as the truck disappeared around the next corner.

Callie's face was pale. "Do you think he's coming back?" she asked.

Frank shook his head. "I don't think there's a place for him to turn around on this road." He looked at the girl slung over Joe's shoulder. "Who do we have here?"

The girl kicked her legs and twisted in Joe's arms. "Put me down! Put me down, you stupid oaf!"

Joe found a soft patch of grass by the iron gate, bent over, and dumped the girl on the ground. "There, you're down," he said.

The girl jumped up and glared at Joe. "Do you know who I am? I am Gabi von Kubiza! My father is Egon von Kubiza. He owns half the country."

"Good," Frank said. "That means we're in the right place." He extended his hand to Gabi. "I'm Frank Hardy." He nodded toward Joe and Callie, introducing them. "We're here to work with Dr. Maxwell for the next week."

"So," Gabi said, lifting her nose in the air, "you are part of that stinking archaeology project my father is wasting his money on."

"I take it you don't share his interest," Callie said.

Gabi waved her hand, dismissing the idea. "No. My father has very expensive fantasies." She turned her attention toward her car. "Look what you have done," she said, surveying the damage. "You made me put another dent in this heap of trash car."

Joe noticed that the hatchback was in pretty sorry shape. The wheel wells were rusted out, plus each of the fenders had at least one dent or scratch. And the passenger door had been caved in when it hit the tree.

"Help me push it free," Gabi said.

"First, you tell me why you tried to get run down," Joe said.

With a sneer, Gabi looked off in the direction the truck had gone and said, "Those cowards would not hit me."

Callie's eyebrows shot up. "You know who was in that truck?"

"Zimmermann Construction," Gabi said. "Since this Dr. Maxwell project started, Herr

Zimmermann has been in a big fight with my father. Zimmermann sends his trucks roaring past our house every hour to try to intimidate us. He is a stupid idiot."

"What's the fight about?" Frank asked.

"*Ach,* I do not know. Just help me get my car going, okay? I am late."

When the Hardys pushed her car back onto the road, Gabi jumped in and took off down the mountain without even a wave.

Egon von Kubiza was a professor of ancient history at the University of Stuttgart and also happened to own one of the largest estates in southern Germany, part of a vast real-estate empire that his family had built over generations. Frank knew from the file that he was wealthy enough to sponsor Dr. Maxwell's research, but his mansion was even more spectacular than the Hardys had imagined.

"It's more of a castle than a house," Callie said as they pulled up the crescent driveway. Built entirely of pale yellow stone, the mansion stood four stories tall, with towers on each corner. The roof was red clay half-pipe, and marble lions guarded the front door.

"Hey, those things are wild," Joe said, looking up as they got out of the car. Gargoyles perched above every window.

"They're supposed to ward off evil spirits," Frank said.

"Good afternoon. You must be Frank and Joe Hardy," a female voice called out.

The teenagers turned and saw a petite young woman with long dark hair come around the corner of the mansion. She wore brown thermal coveralls and muddy hiking boots. "I'm Stephi Bijazet," the woman said, shaking hands firmly all around. "I'm Dr. Maxwell's research assistant. Welcome to Germany." She used her hand to shade her eyes and peeked into the Porsche. "I thought there were supposed to be four of you."

"Right," Joe said. "My girlfriend, Vanessa, was coming, but she stayed home to help her mom with a huge computer project."

"Well, she's going to miss an exciting discovery," Stephi said, leading them through the oak double doors of the mansion.

"You think you're getting close to finding the fort?" Frank asked.

"Any day now," Stephi answered. "Especially now that you're here to help out."

"I could get used to living here," Joe said as they stepped inside. Two full suits of armor flanked the door, each holding a double-bladed battle-ax. An enormous crystal chandelier hung from the cathedral ceiling. Instead of wallpaper, murals of medieval Europe were hand-painted on the walls.

"This is amazing," Callie said. "How old are those murals?"

"I'd guess at least a hundred years," Stephi

said. "This house has been in Herr von Kubiza's family for centuries. He's been very kind. We use the carriage house out back as our research center, and tonight he's even planned a New Year's Eve dinner to welcome you."

The teenagers deposited their luggage in their bedrooms upstairs, then followed Stephi out back to the carriage house. It was a two-story building with a marble fountain in front.

Inside, the carriage house felt to Frank like a cross between a modern office and a war room. The desk in the front room had Stephi's name on it. Books littered the whole place, and white posterboard and detailed charts covered the walls. However, the painting on the side wall above Stephi's desk immediately captured Frank's attention.

The oil painting showed a golden shield with walnut-size blue sapphires in the corners and diamonds and amethysts along the edges. In the center was a dragon formed from thousands of tiny emeralds. The dragon spit ruby flames from its mouth.

"Emperor Decius's shield," Frank said.

Callie went over to the painting and gazed at it. "The actual shield must be worth a fortune," she murmured.

"Priceless," Stephi agreed. "A real treasure. It's hard to believe it's been buried right around here somewhere for nearly two thousand years."

"Yeah, you'd think someone would have found it by now," Frank said.

"Many have tried," Stephi said. "Let's go upstairs and meet your dad's old roommate. We just got back from the field a little while ago."

Dr. John Maxwell looked exactly as Fenton Hardy had described him to his sons. He wore a dingy gray tweed overcoat and old beat-up duck boots, and had a thick shock of wild black hair that made his head look sort of lopsided, as if he'd slept on it wrong. Though he was the same age as Fenton, Dr. Maxwell looked much older.

As soon as he saw the Hardys, Dr. Maxwell threw down the sheaf of papers he was reading and strode over.

"You must be Joe," he said to Frank in a soft voice.

"I'm Frank."

That information seemed to pass right through Dr. Maxwell. "And you must be Frank," he said, pointing a bony finger at Joe.

"No," Stephi said firmly. She pointed to each brother and said their names. "And this is their friend Callie Shaw."

"Yes, right, right," Dr. Maxwell said. "Absolutely. Wonderful to have you here." Dr. Maxwell's eyes went up to the ceiling for a moment as though he were lost in thought. "Yes, it's terrific to finally meet you. Did you make it here okay from the airport? Is your father still in the private detective business? Hmmm?"

Frank and Joe exchanged glances. This guy was out there. " 'Yes' to both questions," Frank said.

"Good, good, good. We're doing some interesting detective work here, too. Let's give you the latest news, okay?" Maxwell suggested.

"Sure," Frank said. He, Joe, and Callie sat in steel folding chairs and watched as Dr. Maxwell shuffled through some computer printouts and Stephi brought over an easel with a map of Köbingen on it.

"You always explain things more clearly than I do," Dr. Maxwell said to Stephi.

Taking her cue, Stephi pointed to a spot on the map just north of Köbingen. "This is Herr von Kubiza's estate," she said. "I assume you saw our notes about the old road."

The three teenagers nodded.

"Well, it only makes sense that a fort would be built on the highest elevation available between the road and the river."

"Sure," Frank pointed out. "It's always easier to defend from an elevated spot."

"Right, right, right," Dr. Maxwell mumbled from the side of the room.

"Okay," Stephi said. "Herr von Kubiza's estate is on the highest mountain, and it borders the river. We thought we'd find the fort here, but after weeks of surveying we haven't found anything. We've checked a few other possibilities. Nothing there, either. The most likely spots left are here and here." She pointed to a spot close to the von Kubiza estate and another spot a few miles away, south of town.

"This estate next to us belongs to Herr Ernst Gipfel," Stephi explained. "For some reason he wouldn't give us permission to work on his land."

"He didn't say why?" Joe asked.

Dr. Maxwell waved his hand in front of his face as if swatting a fly. "He's just a crazy old lunatic," he said. "He doesn't need a reason."

Stephi smiled. "This spot south of town belongs to Herr Zimmermann. He owns a construction company and plans to build a shopping mall here."

The Hardys didn't mention their recent adventure with the Zimmermann truck.

"Herr Zimmermann has millions of dollars invested in this land," Stephi explained. "If we find the fort there, he won't be able to develop the land, and he could lose all that money."

Callie leaned forward in her chair. "So he won't let you look on his land either, right?"

Dr. Maxwell interrupted again. "But we've taken care of both of them," he said. "The city council has just given us the right of prospect wherever we want. And there's a construction ban for all of Köbingen until we're through. Herr von Kubiza has some very powerful friends, you see."

"There's still a couple of hours of daylight left," Frank said. "I'm ready to get started."

"That's the spirit!" Dr. Maxwell lifted his arms

in the air. "You sound just like Fenton Hardy's son. Stephi, call Herr Gipfel and tell him we're on our way."

After a brief argument between Stephi and Dr. Maxwell about the next place to start the search, and a quick stop in the kitchen of the von Kubiza mansion to get Joe a sandwich and an apple to snack on, the Hardys and Callie soon found themselves on Ernst Gipfel's estate.

Frank helped Stephi unload crates of equipment from the back of the big, mud-splattered, white four-wheel-drive van. He could see von Kubiza's mansion over on the next ridge, about a mile away.

"We should be working the Zimmermann land," Stephi said under her breath.

"You think so?" Frank lifted a box of T-shaped wire sensors from the back of the van.

Stephi tossed the long-handled soil sample tool to the ground behind her and unrolled a survey map, holding it up for Frank to see. "That's the next obvious place," she said, pointing. "There's a bend in the river there, and the cliffs make it a perfect lookout spot."

"I'm sure we'll get to it," Frank said calmly.

"You're right. I just wish Dr. Maxwell would listen to me for once." Stephi placed a steel box pocked with dials and electrical contact points on top of the case in Frank's arms. "Take this out to that tree," she said, pointing to a huge old oak tree about a hundred yards away.

Frank, Joe, and Callie each grabbed a handful of the T-shaped electrode probes from Frank's box. Under Dr. Maxwell's direction, they attached copper wiring to clips under the insulated handles at the top of each probe and ran the wires back to an array of batteries at the van. Then, starting at the oak tree, they placed the two-foot-long probes in the ground, carefully spacing them at one-meter intervals.

Joe had to twist one probe to get it to sink to the proper depth in the frozen soil. "I thought we'd be doing some digging," he said to Frank.

"You didn't read the file, did you?" Frank joked. "This is called resistivity prospecting. When we tell Stephi to throw the switch, an electrical current will go through these probes and into the ground. They'll measure the electrical resistance of the soil."

Callie chimed in as she stepped ahead to place the next wire. "If there's anything important under there, it'll show up on the graphs in the van."

"Got it, Professor," Joe said.

Frank checked the wires on his last two probes. He thought he heard Dr. Maxwell cough, and looked up.

It was no cough—it was a growl. Two huge German shepherds were racing toward them from Gipfel's house, growling and baring their teeth.

The guard dogs stopped about ten yards away, barking ferociously. Frank could feel his pulse quicken. As he stepped in front of Callie, the dogs flattened their ears and charged.

Chapter

3

FRANK STARTED TO TOSS the wires aside. He knew the German shepherds would go for his throat, which meant he had to keep his chin down and try to fend them off using his forearms and fists.

With a few powerful bounds the dogs were upon him. At the last second Frank dropped to his knees. "Hit the juice, Stephi!" he yelled toward the van.

The electrodes hummed in his hands. Frank saw the dogs leap into the air, their bared fangs glistening with strands of saliva. He braced himself like a fullback about to take a hit and thrust the electric probes forward.

He caught one dog in the neck, the other in

the chest. There was a sizzling sound, and sparks exploded in every direction. Even through the insulated handles, Frank could feel a charge shooting up his arms, but he didn't let go.

With a strangled yelp the dogs fell to the ground, twitching. The smell of scorched fur lingered in the air.

Frank dropped the electrodes and knelt beside the dogs. Joe and Callie joined him.

Dr. Maxwell walked over with his long, loping strides and clapped Frank on the back. "That was quick thinking."

"What happened?" Stephi was breathless after running over from the van.

"Guard dogs," Joe said. He pressed his fingers against the neck of the nearest dog. The pulse was faint but rapid. "Frank stunned them with the electrodes, but they'll be okay."

"I can't believe this," Stephi said. She pulled her hair back behind her ears as she bent over the dogs. "I called Gipfel before we left the house to tell him we were coming."

Frank saw Dr. Maxwell's expression harden. The scientist, with his tall, angular frame, loomed over Stephi like a specter. "Did you actually speak to Gipfel?" he asked.

Stephi took a step back. "I left a message on his machine," she said defensively.

"Then it's no wonder the dogs were still out, is it?"

"It's okay," Frank said. "Nobody got hurt."

24

"Yeah," Joe added, "but these two mutts aren't going to stay down for more than a few minutes. I say we tie them to the nearest tree."

Dr. Maxwell's anger seemed to disappear as quickly as it had come. "Good thinking. We still have time to take these measurements. Stephi, get some rope from the van."

With the German shepherds out of the way, the prospecting proceeded without incident. The dogs recovered after a while but seemed too tired to bark much. Stephi worked in the field with Callie and Joe, checking coordinates and directing the placement of the probes, while Frank stayed in the van with Dr. Maxwell.

The instruments used to measure the electrical current flowing through the ground were arranged in a row on a shelf in the back of the van.

"These things look like seismographs or lie detectors," Frank said, watching the needles jitter across reams of computer paper. On the other wall of the van, color computer monitors registered waves of bending color.

"Yes," Dr. Maxwell said, cupping his chin with one hand as he watched the data flow in. "We're getting some good readings today. The soil is moist and cold. That's good."

Frank heard Stephi call, "Give us some juice!" and he threw the switch to send out the current. At Dr. Maxwell's signal, he shut it off. "Can you tell from these readings what's under there?" he asked.

"No, no," Dr. Maxwell said dreamily, as if mesmerized by the jagged lines and flowing colors. "Not unless something really huge and conductive, like a battleship, were buried out there. We'll have to analyze this information back at the house."

"That's where the Geographical Information Systems technology comes in, right?" Frank said.

Dr. Maxwell smiled, and said, "You do know something about archaeology." They waited for the next signal from Stephi, then Dr. Maxwell continued. "My GIS programs allow us to overlay one type of information on another."

"Right," Frank said. "You take these electrical readings and make a map out of them. Then you lay that map over a map of soil samples, topography, infrared, whatever."

"Yes, yes. You've got it. All that information allows us to see much more than we used to be able to." Dr. Maxwell seemed lost in thought again for a moment, then he jumped as if startled. "I think we should break into two teams tomorrow," he said, his eyes lighting up. "We'll cover twice the area. How does that sound?"

"Sounds excellent," Frank said, growing excited at the prospect. Dr. Maxwell's enthusiasm for his project was contagious.

The Hardys and Callie finally met Egon von Kubiza when they returned to the mansion at dusk. He was short and powerfully built, like a wrestler, and wore wire-rimmed glasses and a thick handlebar mustache. After welcoming the visitors at the front door and reminding them to be ready for dinner in two hours, he and Dr. Maxwell disappeared into the carriage house. They planned to download the data from the field equipment to the research computers.

Stephi looked disappointed.

"What's wrong?" Callie asked, following Frank and Joe into the mansion.

Stephi jammed her hands into the pockets of her coveralls. "Nothing. It's just that I'd like to see what we picked up today. But it's better to stay out of the way when those two get together."

"They get pretty excited, huh?" Callie said.

"I can't get a word in edgewise," Stephi said as they climbed up the four flights of marble stairs. "It's as if I'm not even there."

The four of them paused at the fourth-floor landing before splitting off to their individual rooms. "Cheer up," Frank said. "Dr. Maxwell was talking this afternoon about splitting us into two groups on our next research trip. You'll get to lead a couple of us around."

Stephi brightened. "That's great news," she said. "I'll finally get the chance to try out some of my theories for once." She smiled and turned down the hall to her room. "See you at dinner."

At exactly eight o'clock Frank, Joe, and Callie descended to the dining room. For the New Year's celebration, the Hardys wore jackets and ties, and

Callie had put on a black cocktail dress. The centerpiece of the room was a twenty-foot-long polished mahogany dining table. Ornate silver candelabra decorated the table and the matching sideboard, and the feast murals on the walls seemed to shimmer in the candlelight. Stephi stood with Gabi in front of a fireplace at the far end of the room. She had replaced her dusty coveralls with a red satin floor-length gown.

Joe cupped his hand over his mouth and whispered to Frank, "Stephi sure looks different, doesn't she?"

Frank adjusted his tie. "I have to agree."

"Cool off, guys," Callie said, tossing her hair over her shoulder and taking Frank's hand. "Let's try to make friends with Gabi again."

But Joe couldn't help himself as he got a closer look at the young woman. "Whose funeral?" he said under his breath, gesturing to Gabi's black dress. Gabi was also wearing her black lipstick and black nail polish.

"Are you back to pester me again?" she said with a surly look at Joe.

"Gabi!" a voice boomed from the next room. "It is New Year's Eve. No more of your angst and unhappiness, okay?" Herr von Kubiza entered dressed in a tuxedo. Dr. Maxwell followed, a big grin on his face.

"Sit down, everyone, please," Herr von Kubiza said. "We have reason to celebrate. We have good food, we have guests visiting from America, and Dr. Maxwell may be very close indeed to finding the Shield of Decius."

"Did we locate something today?" Stephi asked, excitement creeping into her voice.

"Sit down, Stephi, sit down," Herr von Kubiza said gently. "Let us relax for a moment."

Frank sympathized with Stephi. He could barely keep himself from asking questions as the plates of food went around and Dr. Maxwell and von Kubiza made small talk.

Joe took two helpings of roast goose and apple-nut stuffing before passing the dish on.

When Herr von Kubiza teased his daughter about the new dent in her car, she said snootily, "You should just buy me another one."

Herr von Kubiza laughed. "I believe you are spoiled. Maybe we should ask our guests what they think, eh?"

Gabi's bracelets made quite a racket as she ate. "I think this whole project is silly," she said. "You are always away digging things up."

"Silly?" Herr von Kubiza took off his glasses and polished them with his napkin. "Julius Caesar built the fort we are searching for during the Gallic wars. The fort is mentioned by the historian Quinctius. Caesar Decius reclaimed it four hundred years later as the Roman Empire was contracting."

Gabi didn't seem impressed.

"This fort is like a miniature history of the entire empire," von Kubiza said earnestly. "General

29

Decius hid his armory here and retreated. He planned to come back the next year as emperor to resume his war against the German people. But he was killed in battle."

"That's why you believe the Köbingen fort contains the shield," Callie said.

Herr von Kubiza nodded as he smiled at Gabi. "I tell you what," he said. "If we find the shield, I'll get you any kind of car you wish."

Gabi looked to Callie. "What is the saying in English? I will not be holding my breath."

Everyone laughed, but Frank couldn't keep quiet anymore. "So what's the news?"

Dr. Maxwell shrugged. "I don't like to get excited prematurely," he said. "But Herr von Kubiza and I may have seen something on the readings we took today at Gipfel's."

Stephi toyed with the gold pendant around her neck. "What did you see?"

"Just some shadows," Dr. Maxwell said.

Herr von Kubiza interrupted. "I brought some additional satellite images back from the university today. They will tell us for sure if we are onto something, yes?"

"Yes, yes," Dr. Maxwell said. "Tomorrow we should have something definitive, one way or the other."

Herr von Kubiza went to the sideboard and returned with a wooden cigar box. "I have a special treat for all of us," he said. "It's a German

New Year's Eve custom called *Bleigiessen.* It predicts your fate for the new year."

He took six tiny lead pellets from the box and dropped them into his spoon. He then held the spoon over one of the candles. "When the metal melts, you tip it into your glass." He turned his wrist and poured his molten lead into the water. A hiss of steam rose from the goblet. "By interpreting the shape, we know what the new year holds in store," he explained.

"It reminds me of the ink blots we read about in psychology class," Callie said. "It's a three-D Rorschach test."

Herr von Kubiza nodded and fished his lead out of the glass. "Let's see what I've got."

It was a half bubble with a stem poking out of the bottom. Joe thought it looked like a palm tree, but before he could open his mouth, Callie said, "It's an umbrella."

"An umbrella," Herr von Kubiza echoed. "Brilliant. Although next year will bring foul weather, I will not be soaked. I could not imagine a better fortune."

Everyone around the table took a turn pouring the lead into a glass of water. According to the oracle, Frank would spend some time on a tropical island. Stephi came up with a car, and Gabi tried to take it from her. Joe found a trophy, which assured many victories during the upcoming basketball and baseball seasons. Callie's fortune looked like a hammer to Frank, but she insisted it was a gavel, which meant she would be elected class president. Frank knew to keep his mouth shut.

They had the most fun with Gabi's fortune. Her father said it looked like an icicle, and Joe commented that it could be a stake. Gabi finally convinced them that it meant her year would be smooth and straight.

At last the lead came around to Dr. Maxwell. "We scientists don't put much faith in this kind of mysticism," he said. He poured the lead in and then studied it, frowning. It resembled a long box with the lid propped open.

Stephi gasped.

"What is it?" Frank asked.

"It's a coffin!" Stephi exclaimed. "He's going to die."

"Hush, Stephi," Herr von Kubiza said.

Callie looked at the lead and said, "This is the wrong shape for a coffin. Too short. It's more of a box."

"A treasure chest," Joe added. "That's exactly what it is." He looked at Dr. Maxwell and said, "Congratulations. You're going to find the shield."

"Perfect," Herr von Kubiza said. "Good fortune for everyone."

Frank was awakened early the next morning by a violent knocking at his door. "Get up," a female voice said urgently. "Are you awake? Get up!"

Frank ran his hands through his hair and checked his travel alarm. It was 5:30 A.M. He cracked his door a few inches. Stephi stood out in the hall, dressed for field work. "What is it?" he asked.

Stephi pushed the door open and thrust a sheet of computer paper into Frank's hand. "Read that," she said. "I'm going to wake the others. This is unbelievable. All our work gone down the drain."

Frank rubbed his eyes, trying to get them to focus. The note was addressed to Stephi.

3:00 A.M., Jan. 1
Stephi,

After careful examination of the new photos Herr von Kubiza brought from the university yesterday, I've come to the painful conclusion that my Theory is incorrect. There is no fort.

I know this is terribly disappointing news for you. I cannot face you or Herr von Kubiza and have decided to leave the country quietly to avoid any further embarrassment.

I'm sorry.
John Maxwell

Chapter

4

WITHIN MINUTES the Hardys, Callie, and Stephi had gathered in Dr. Maxwell's tiny bedroom on the second floor of the carriage house. Even Gabi showed up, her blue hair still spiked as if she hadn't slept on it at all.

"What is all the noise?" she asked. "New Year's Day is for sleeping in."

"For the first time, I agree with you," Joe said, rubbing his hands together. He'd forgotten to put on his coat, and the carriage house was freezing cold.

"We're just a little concerned about Dr. Maxwell," Frank said to Gabi. "Is your father around?"

"No. He is already gone—doing his research,"

34

she said bitterly. "He leaves for the university by five in the morning, even on holidays."

Stephi walked to the closet and brushed her hand against the empty coat hangers. They banged together like chimes in a storm. "I can't believe Dr. Maxwell would just leave like this. And the van is still outside."

Joe took the note from Frank. "This says three A.M.," he said. "That was only a few hours ago."

"Yeah, he can't be far." Frank gestured to the books and papers stacked on the desk and floor. "Stephi, we need to find out what Dr. Maxwell discovered that made him decide so suddenly that his theories were a bust."

Callie stepped out of the bathroom holding a toiletry kit in one hand and an old sock in the other. "He must have packed in a hurry to have forgotten his toothbrush," she said.

Stephi shook her head. "That's just like him," she said. "Dr. Maxwell is pretty forgetful."

"Okay," Frank said. "Stephi, keep checking through the papers." He glanced at his watch. "It's six in the morning here, so it's midnight back in Bayport. Callie, call my dad. No wait." Frank didn't want to upset Dr. Maxwell's family before he had an idea of what was going on. "Just E-mail Dad," he said. "Ask him to find out tomorrow if Dr. Maxwell contacted his family."

"What about me?" Gabi asked, crossing her arms in front of her chest.

"If you really want to help," Joe said, "you

could call the taxi companies to see if they picked him up."

Stephi sat down at one of the computers and pointed out, "The train station is within walking distance."

"You think he'd walk, even with all his luggage?" Frank asked.

Stephi sighed. "No, I guess not."

"Well, see what you can find out." Frank turned to his brother. "Joe, let's go talk to the staff to find out if anyone saw anything."

The staff quarters was a row of rooms off the back of the main house near the kitchen. The rooms had a perfect view of the carriage house. Joe knocked on the first door. After a few minutes the maid answered, wrapped in her robe.

"Ja?" she said, a puzzled look on her face.

"Entschuldigen Sie," Frank said, apologizing for waking her up. "Do you speak English?"

"Ja, er . . . yes, a little. You are the two American boys, yes?"

"Right," Joe said, trying to sound casual and unconcerned. "We were looking for Dr. Maxwell. Have you seen him around?"

The maid looked annoyed. "You wake me up for this? Herr von Kubiza sent you?"

"No," Frank said.

"You people," the maid said, clutching at the neck of her robe. "First that crazy scientist keeps me awake half the night. Such a racket comes

36

from the carriage house. Now you come wake me up this early?"

"It's important," Frank said. "What did you hear last night?"

"I was asleep. Then a loud crash woke me up. I looked out my window and saw Dr. Maxwell standing by his van. He must have dropped something, but what kind of work can you do at two o'clock in the morning?"

"What was he doing?" Joe asked.

"I don't know. I just tried to go back to sleep."

The maid began to shut the door, but Joe gently held it open, and asked, "Just one other thing. Was anyone else with him?"

"I heard some voices, perhaps. I just wish to sleep."

"Male or female?" Frank asked, but he was too late. The door slammed shut in his face.

No one answered when they knocked on the other two doors. "Come on." Frank led the way out the back door and into the area between the mansion and the carriage house. "Let's take a look around the van," he said.

Joe shivered as the icy wind whipped at his T-shirt. The sun was coming up, bleeding a red tint into the thick fog hanging in the valley between the Gipfel and von Kubiza estates.

"It looks as if someone drove the van last night," Frank said. "I remember us parking farther down the drive when we came back yesterday."

"You think Dr. Maxwell went out prospecting by himself?" Joe knelt down and checked around the back of the van for debris.

"I don't know," Frank said. "Maybe he found a flaw in his theory and couldn't wait to test it out. That would explain his leaving at three A.M."

"Look at this." Joe stood up and showed Frank what he'd found—a strip of metal about two inches long, some strange-looking chunks of glass, and a few shards of black plastic.

Frank took the strip of metal and hefted it. "Some sort of alloy. It won't bend at all."

"Look at the way this glass is broken," Joe said. "It's in perfectly geometrical pieces."

"It might be quartz, not glass," Frank noted.

Joe was holding the fragments up to the pale light of the sunrise when he heard a heavily accented voice behind him ask, "Is there something wrong with Dr. Maxwell's van?"

The Hardys turned. Two burly men dressed in heavy wool coats and gray knit ski caps emerged from the fog and walked up the hill toward them. The bigger of the two men was well over six feet tall. He carried a pickax over his shoulder and wore a cap stained with sweat. The smaller man carried a shovel.

The Hardys hastily stuffed the evidence in their pockets.

"I am Karl, the cook," the smaller man said, stopping a few paces in front of Frank and Joe. "And this is Johann, our mechanic. He fixes things." Karl stuck the blade of his shovel in the ground and leaned on the handle. "If there is something wrong with the van, Johann can make it work."

"No, there's nothing wrong," Frank said. "Herr von Kubiza has you out early this morning."

"Yes," Karl said. He looked over his shoulder. "We were just mending the fence down by Herr Gipfel's estate."

"You didn't happen to see Dr. Maxwell around earlier, did you?" Joe asked.

"No, we did not see anything." Karl said something to Johann in German, and Johann laughed and shook his head.

"He's laughing because you're out here in just a T-shirt," Frank said to Joe.

"Ah, so you speak German," Karl said. "Very good. Most Americans know only English."

Frank nodded.

"Are you sure there is nothing wrong with the van?" Karl asked, picking up his shovel and stepping close to look behind the Hardys.

"Nothing at all," Frank said.

Karl and Johann headed toward the staff quarters. "Don't miss breakfast," Karl called. "I'm cooking up some German specialties for you."

After the two men disappeared inside, Frank motioned for Joe to follow him. They walked downhill toward Gipfel's property, the frosted ground crunching under their feet.

"What is it?" Joe asked.

"Karl got me to thinking about something. Let me see Dr. Maxwell's note."

Joe handed it over.

" 'Stephi,' " Frank read aloud. " 'After careful examination of the new photos Herr von Kubiza brought from the university yesterday, I've come to the painful conclusion that my Theory is incorrect. . . .' Look," Frank said. "*Theory* is capitalized."

"Yeah, so?"

"So, think about it. All nouns are capitalized in written German, not just names and other proper nouns. Capitalizing *Theory* isn't a mistake an English speaker would make."

"So Dr. Maxwell might not have written this note?"

"Right."

"I don't know, Frank. Dr. Maxwell's pretty goofy. He doesn't seem like he's too worried about little grammatical details. Besides, the other nouns aren't capitalized."

"Maybe you're right. But ask yourself two questions: Who wasn't too keen on this project? And where did Dr. Maxwell go last night?"

"Herr Gipfel and Herr Gipfel's estate," Joe answered.

"And here we are," Frank said.

A whitewashed three-board fence stretched out in front of them. On the other side Herr Gipfel's apple orchard spread across the rest of the valley and up the next hill. The trees were bare, sticking up from the ground like black, skeletal hands. Frank jumped the fence and Joe followed.

"Watch out for Lassie and Rin Tin Tin," Joe said, keeping an eye out for the German shepherd guard dogs.

Frank led the way up a dirt path. After about half a mile of climbing, they reached an old house constructed of exposed half-timbers. It was narrow, but four stories tall. The entire structure listed to one side, as if it might topple at any second.

A sign hung on the iron gate at the beginning of the front walk. It read *Betreten Verboten.*

"What's it mean?" Joe asked.

"It says come on in and make yourselves at home. Fridge is full."

"Yeah, right."

"Come on. Let's see what we can find before we formally introduce ourselves." Frank scaled the iron gate and dropped down on the other side.

Joe dropped down next to his brother. The two of them crept up to the house, staying close to the bushes lining the walk.

"The car's here," Joe whispered, pointing to an older model black Mercedes sedan in the driveway.

Frank motioned for Joe to follow him as he approached the front door. It was decorated with a heavy cast-iron knocker shaped like a gargoyle.

Joe came up next to Frank and peered through the square window cut high in the door. "It's too dark," he said. "I can't see anything in there."

Frank placed his hand on the door knocker to brace himself as he looked in. Something clicked. He heard the squeaking sound of a pulley and looked up—too late. He was yanked off his feet and felt himself rocket into the air.

Chapter

5

FRANK HEARD JOE YELL as the two of them collided in a human knot, swinging like a pendulum six feet in the air. A thick rope pressed into Frank's face. When he looked down, he realized they'd been swooped up and captured in a giant net.

Joe struggled, fighting against the grip of the net. The rope burned his palms as he tried to pull himself upright, but it was no use. He couldn't get his footing as he and his brother swayed back and forth. They were helpless.

"Are you okay?" Frank asked. He could feel Joe's elbow digging into his back.

"I wish I had my knife," Joe grumbled.

Below them, a deep, menacing voice said,

"There is an old saying: If wishes were horses, then beggars would ride."

Joe wrenched his head around and caught a glimpse of a metallic arm grabbing the handle of a winch. With three blunt, steel fingers, the man-made hand cranked the handle of the winch next to the door.

As the net began descending, Joe could see that the prosthetic arm was attached to a human shoulder—a big one. The guy was about the same height as Joe, but built like an Olympic weight lifter, with a huge barrel chest and a belly that looked flabby but was probably rock hard.

"Who are you?" Frank asked.

The man stopped turning the winch, and the net swung two feet off the ground. "This is what I should be asking you, my young American friend."

"We'd prefer to speak on the ground," Joe said.

"And perhaps I'd prefer to let you hang there until you freeze," the man replied.

"All right," Frank said. He figured he and Joe could take the guy if they needed to once they were back on the ground. "I'm Frank Hardy, and this is my brother, Joe. We're working with Dr. Maxwell and Herr von Kubiza."

"That is better. I am Ernst Gipfel." The man then cranked them down, and they scrambled out of the net.

With the ground finally under his feet, Frank

could see how the contraption worked. The weave of the rope net fit the pattern of the flagstones on the front walk. The rope virtually disappeared as it slid into place between the stones. High above the doorway, a gargoyle housed the pulley in its mouth.

Herr Gipfel finished winding the winch with his three-fingered hand. He then turned and glowered at the Hardys. "Are you going to tell me what you're doing here, or do I need to call the police?"

"We just came to ask you a few questions," Joe said, shivering. "Do you mind if we go inside?"

Eyeing them suspiciously, Herr Gipfel opened the door and made a sweeping motion with his arm. "This way."

Joe stepped inside, the wooden floor squeaking under his feet. The first thing he spotted was someone hiding in the corner holding an ice ax. Gipfel switched on the light before Joe could react. Joe then realized the arm holding the ax wasn't attached to a body. It was mounted on the wall. For a moment he thought he'd be sick. Frank stared at it, too.

Gipfel took off his jacket and hung it over the arm. "*Ja, ja.* This was my original arm. They packed it in ice after the climbing accident, but the doctor could not reattach it. I had it taxidermied into a coatrack."

He held up his mechanical arm and snapped

the steel fingers into a fist. "I like the new one better anyway. Strong as a vise," Gipfel said, sitting down in a wing chair by the fireplace. "So, tell me why you are here. Is it not enough that that thief Egon von Kubiza gets to search my land without my permission?"

The Hardys remained standing. "I take it you and Herr von Kubiza aren't friends?" Frank stated.

Herr Gipfel stood and began rearranging some small statuettes on the fireplace mantel. "Egon is not an archaeologist," he said. "He just wants to dig up the artifacts and sell them to the highest bidder. I heard he did just that in Turkey."

"Dr. Maxwell is a close friend of our father," Joe said. "He's an honorable man, not the kind to do anything wrong."

"We shall see," Herr Gipfel said, returning to his chair. "The city council may let you work on my property, but I do not have to trust your Dr. Maxwell. I plan to keep an eye on him. And I have my own plans for the fort." He stared at the fireplace, and the flames made odd shadows float across his face.

"It's Dr. Maxwell who brings us here," Frank said, carefully watching Gipfel for a telltale sign of guilt. "We wondered if you'd seen him around."

"No," Gipfel said. He stood up and poked at the fire. "Are you saying Dr. Maxwell is missing?"

"No," Joe said. "We're only saying . . ." He

tried to think of a way to put it without giving too much away.

Frank interrupted. "We had a little encounter with your dogs yesterday, and we were just concerned for Dr. Maxwell. He may have come back here late last night."

"My dogs? What is this? Are you accusing me of something?" Herr Gipfel stepped toward Frank, swiping at him with his steel arm. "Get out! Get out of my house!"

Frank stood his ground, and Joe braced himself, ready for anything.

Gipfel stopped, his red face inches from Frank's, like a baseball coach shouting at an umpire. "I have not seen Dr. Maxwell, but I will tell you where he is. I think he has already found the shield and smuggled it back to America. I suspected it all along."

Frank stayed totally calm. "I'm sure that's not true."

"It *is* true," Herr Gipfel said, his whole body trembling with indignation. "Now go."

Frank and Joe excused themselves politely and left. They didn't speak to each other until Gipfel's house was out of sight.

"He sure doesn't like Herr von Kubiza," Frank said.

"Can you believe that stuffed arm?" Joe rubbed his shoulder as if it were in pain. "Anyone as twisted as Gipfel should stay at the top of our suspect list."

"That's only if our hunch is correct and something bad happened to Dr. Maxwell."

"You don't think Gipfel would deliberately do something to stop the research?" Joe asked.

"He pretty much admitted that he would," Frank noted. "But Herr Gipfel isn't our only suspect. Remember, Zimmermann Construction has a beef against Herr von Kubiza, too."

Joe nodded. "And Stephi seems awfully ambitious. An archaeological find like this could make her famous."

"We need to keep quiet about our suspicions for now," Frank said. "We'll retrace Dr. Maxwell's steps to see if he discovered something about the fort that got him in trouble."

Back at the mansion the Hardys found Callie and Stephi sitting at a round, glass-topped table in the breakfast room. They looked tired and glum.

"Where have you two been?" Callie asked.

"Just out looking around," Frank replied. He sat down, and Stephi pushed over a cup of hot cocoa. "The maid saw Dr. Maxwell at around two A.M. We can assume he was out prospecting," Frank said.

Stephi slapped her hand down on the table. "I can't believe Dr. Maxwell would go out in the field without me. We were a team."

As Joe sat down he remembered that the maid had said she might have heard Dr. Maxwell talking to someone. He wondered if that might have been Stephi, but he kept quiet. Instead, he studied his plate. In the center was a tiny, colorful knit ski cap, something a doll might wear. He lifted it by the red tassel and found an egg underneath. "The eggs here seem to be as cold as I am," he said, laughing. "By the way, where's my good friend, Gabi?"

"She bailed on us and went back to bed," Callie said. "We haven't had much luck since you left."

Frank sipped his cocoa and buttered a slice of bread. "What's up?"

Stephi spoke in a dull monotone: "No taxi came to pick up Dr. Maxwell. Callie E-mailed your father. The airlines won't give us any information over the phone. The police won't take a missing person report until after twenty-four hours have passed. And most of Dr. Maxwell's notes and computer files are either gone or erased."

"We did find this," Callie said, handing Frank a white envelope. "It's a bill from an aerial photography company in Stuttgart."

"You think this company took the photos Herr von Kubiza brought back from the university yesterday afternoon?" Frank asked.

"Yes," Stephi said. "Dr. Maxwell and I wanted something with more detail than the satellite images we had. But Dr. Maxwell must have taken the photos with him, because we can't find them anywhere."

Joe stacked slices of cheese and cold cuts on a roll. "Time for another drive in the Porsche," he said.

The readings they'd taken at Gipfel's were missing as well, so Frank decided to return there with Stephi and Callie to get some new measurements. Joe drove to Stuttgart to investigate the missing photos.

The younger Hardy arrived at the Stuttgart airport just before noon. He found the aerial photography company in a small, windowless hangar next to the main terminal. Two single-propeller planes with matching red stripes down the fuselage sat parked at the far end of the hangar. The pilot's door to one of the planes was open.

When he peered into the plane, Joe saw a wiry, gray-haired man hunched over a piece of equipment behind the seats. Luckily, the man spoke almost perfect English.

"I'm Peter. How can I help you?" he asked after shaking Joe's hand.

"I need to have some pictures taken," Joe said. "Are you free this afternoon?"

The man smiled. "Not free," he said, taking Joe literally. "It'll cost you, but I can take whatever photos you need."

"I work for Herr von Kubiza," Joe said, introducing himself.

"Ah, yes. More photos for von Kubiza. That will be no problem." Peter stepped nimbly between the two front seats of the airplane and jumped to the cement next to Joe. The pockets of his green flight suit were stuffed with pens, maps, and tiny notebooks.

"I need a repeat of whatever you did yesterday afternoon," Joe said.

"What? I didn't do it right the first time?"

"No. You did great. But we seem to have misplaced all those pictures," Joe said.

Taking a map from his breast pocket and a notebook from a pocket at the side of his thigh, Peter walked over to a tall cabinet against the wall. "So you need black-and-white near infrared shots of plots G-16 and Z-20 to Z-30, yes?"

"Yes," Joe said, pretending he knew what Peter was talking about. "That's it exactly."

"Okay," Peter said, pulling several boxes of film from the cabinet. "Let's go."

"I can go up with you?"

"Sure. Maybe you will learn a thing or two." The man smiled easily. "And if you see how hard I work, maybe you won't lose these photos."

The man had loaded the film into a complicated-looking camera that pointed down through a plastic bubble in the belly of the plane. Within minutes Joe was strapped into the passenger seat, and they were airborne. The tiny airplane bucked and swayed against the turbulent air currents.

Peter explained how he could move the camera and take pictures by remote control. A computer screen no bigger than a hand-held calculator showed the terrain below in black and white. Orange crosshairs marked where the camera was pointing.

They flew up toward Köbingen from the south, shooting photos of the Zimmermann property first. It was a long stretch of flat land high on a cliff at a bend in the river. Joe could see bulldozers and backhoes sitting next to a trailer.

They then flew north, to the Gipfel estate. Once there, Peter dropped to a thousand feet and handed Joe a joystick. "Here, you take the pictures," he said. "I'll give you a discount."

"What do I do?"

"Just push that red button when I tell you."

From his window Joe could see Gipfel's house. Ahead, if he shaded his eyes from the glare, he could see Herr von Kubiza's stone mansion.

"Are those your friends?" Peter asked.

Joe spotted the van. Then he saw Callie and Stephi standing close to the huge old oak tree. Peter said, "Mark!" and Joe pushed the button. They went around again, shooting pictures the whole time. Callie and Stephi looked like figurines from a toy train set from Joe's perspective. He figured Frank must be in the van taking the readings.

Then Joe saw another person—much larger than the girls—step out of the shade of the tree. Was that Frank? A flash of light reflected off the figure. No. It was Gipfel, with his metallic arm lifted toward the airplane.

Peter dipped the wings as they were about to

come around for one final pass, and Joe saw Callie wave back.

The plane bucked hard once, and the engine sputtered. Joe looked ahead and saw the propeller stop.

Peter frantically tried to restart the engine, pushing the choke switch again and again.

Nothing.

"Hold on!" Peter yelled as the plane lost speed.

The nose dropped, and the plane went into a steep dive, the earth rushing toward them in a blur.

Chapter

6

PETER PULLED BACK HARD on the stick, trying to raise the nose of the plane. *"Nicht gut!"* he yelled. "My controls are frozen!"

The plane dived faster, and the ground filled the entire windshield. Reaching to his left, Joe flipped a switch, activating the copilot controls. He grabbed the stick and yanked with all his strength.

The nose of the plane came up a little, and Joe could make out individual branches of the barren apple trees ahead.

"We're going to crash!" Peter yelled.

Joe kept pulling. Just as he was sure he'd failed, the nose came up and the plane swooped out of the dive. Tree branches scraped the belly

54

of the plane as Joe steered it along the ridge toward the mountain road.

Peter still clutched at his dead controls, tense with fear, while Joe struggled to pilot the plane. Without power, they could only glide.

"I think we have enough speed to get to the road," Joe said.

They glided silently past Herr von Kubiza's mansion and toward the cliffs. Joe glanced over at Peter. "Try to get the engine started."

Peter composed himself. He started flipping switches and pulling off panels. They were over the road, gliding no more than thirty feet off the ground.

"I'm going to try to bring it down," Joe said, easing off the stick. "I don't see any cars ahead, and this is the only part of the road straight enough for a landing. We've got to go down now."

They were close enough to the road for Joe to see the plane's shadow leading them along. Just as he was about to drop the plane to the pavement, Peter cried out, "There's a car!"

Joe pulled back, but they had no speed. A gust of wind hit the plane from the side, and all of a sudden they were off the road and out over the cliff, two hundred feet above the Neckar River.

"We can go maybe a mile before we hit water," Joe said. "If the cliffs drop before then, maybe we can find a place to land." He couldn't see an end to the high walls on both sides of them.

Peter dug around under the plane's dash some more. He exposed a couple of wires and touched them together. The engine coughed, then died.

The ripples in the water became visible. Joe put one hand on the buckle of his seat belt so he could release it when they hit the river.

Just when Joe thought their luck was running out, Peter touched two more wires together and the engine roared to life. The controls got light in Joe's hands.

"Nice going," Joe said. He flew the plane back up to altitude. Soon they were high over the autobahn, going about the same speed as the cars in the fast lane.

"You know how to fly," Peter said, relief showing on his sweat-slicked face. "That's a good thing." He grabbed the mike. "I'll radio Stuttgart, tell them we're coming in. I just hope we make it."

Joe looked down at the ground passing under them. "So do I," he said, but he was thinking about seeing Gipfel at the site. He hoped Frank and the girls weren't in trouble.

Herr Gipfel had come walking down the hill from his house as soon as Frank, Callie, and Stephi arrived. Gipfel seemed calmer than the day before, even helpful. Frank had to admit that the man knew a lot about German history, but he still didn't trust him. Frank left the rear door of the van open so he could listen to what went on outside, just in case.

He could hear a small plane buzzing overhead, and then he heard Stephi call for power. He pushed a button and sent the electricity through to the probes. The instruments scratched out the data on the computer paper.

While he waited for Stephi's next signal, Frank reached into his pocket for the strip of metal Joe had found under the van. He opened several crates of prospecting equipment stacked on the floor of the van, but didn't see anything the strip fit onto. The last crate contained cylinders that looked like black plastic coffee cans.

"Frank!"

He turned to see Callie standing at the back of the van, pointing up at the sky.

"Frank!" she cried. "Look!"

He saw a single-engine plane silently skim across the tops of the apple trees and disappear into the valley.

"It's the plane taking photographs for us," Callie said. "All of a sudden it just dropped from the sky."

Frank jumped from the back of the van and sprinted to the driver's door. As he spun the van around toward the main road, Gipfel yanked open the passenger door and jumped in.

"What are you doing!" Frank shouted.

"This way," the German said, pointing to a rutted path. "Go behind my house. It's quicker."

Frank followed the path, glancing down into the valley every few seconds to search for wreckage. Soon they bounced out onto the shoulder of the mountain road and skidded to a stop. Frank checked the road in both directions. "I don't see it anywhere," he said.

"The pilot must have gotten it restarted," Gipfel said, shading his eyes with his artificial arm.

"Or else he pulled an incredible stunt."

"Yes, that was quite a dive," Herr Gipfel agreed. "I thought I was going to have quite a mess to clean up in my apple orchard."

After driving a few miles down the road to make sure the plane hadn't gone down nearby, Frank turned the van around and started back to the site. "So, why are you so interested in helping us out today?" he asked. "I thought you were upset with the way we were doing things."

"I am very interested in the Roman fort," Gipfel said. "I am just not so fond of the people in charge of the project." He braced himself against the dash as the van rumbled back onto his property and down toward the big oak tree. "Perhaps I just wish to see that the search—if there is still reason for a search—is conducted correctly, yes?"

"We're doing the best we can, considering Dr. Maxwell isn't around."

"Yes, I believe you are," Herr Gipfel said. He reached into his coat pocket and withdrew a small manila envelope. "These are tickets to the

Schneefest in Esslingen. I want you to have them as a measure of my goodwill."

Frank nodded as he took the envelope. *"Schneefest* means 'snow party,' right?"

"Very good. It is our winter carnival. Folk music and games and plenty of food. It goes on all this week."

"We'll see," Frank said as he stepped out of the van. "I mean, thanks. But we have a lot of work to do."

"Take one evening out for fun," Gipfel said. He bowed slightly to the girls and then trudged up the hill to his house.

A cold wind whipped Callie's hair around her worried face as she asked, "What happened, Frank?"

"Nothing," Frank said. "The pilot must have gotten the plane restarted. And Herr Gipfel has turned out to be very cool all of a sudden."

Frank started pulling the electrodes from the ground and putting them away. "Come on. Let's go analyze this data."

When the three arrived back at the mansion, Herr von Kubiza was waiting for them. His face was red, and he twisted the ends of his mustache nervously as he paced the marble floor of the entrance hall.

"I cannot believe this!" von Kubiza cried. "Gabi told me Dr. Maxwell has abandoned the search. How can this be true?"

Frank, Callie, and Stephi stood against a wall

decorated with a mural of a blacksmith shoeing a horse. Frank felt as if he were facing a firing squad. All he could do was listen to von Kubiza's tirade.

"After all the money I spent proving Dr. Maxwell's theories were correct," Herr von Kubiza continued. "That man has lost his senses. What will I do now?"

"We hope to hear from Dr. Maxwell soon," Frank said, trying to sound reassuring.

"Yes," Stephi added. "And until then we're continuing the fieldwork."

"How can we proceed without Dr Maxwell?" von Kubiza cried. He made a dismissive gesture with his hands. "*Ach*, do what you wish. Keep looking and tell me any news. I must go lie down."

Late that afternoon Frank and Stephi sat in the upstairs room of the carriage house, analyzing the data on a computer. Callie hovered over them, waiting for the results. The room was silent except for the tapping on the keyboard and the hum of the radiator.

"Got it," Stephi said, leaning back in her chair.

Frank and Callie watched a series of multicolored waves appear on the monitor.

"What's that mean?" Callie asked.

"Dirt," Stephi replied, her voice sinking.

"Dirt?"

"Yeah," Frank said, slumping down in his

chair. He traced the lines on the display with his index finger. "Just dirt. These waves represent the natural strata. Any man-made structures would come up geometric. Walls, roofs, foundations—they all have straight lines."

"Hey, look," Stephi said, sitting up. "That might be something."

Frank paged through the topographical maps on the desk. "Go back a couple of frames."

Stephi hit a few keys, and the waves reversed themselves.

"There," Frank said. He pointed to two long, thin areas of elevation among the waves. "Freeze it."

The waves stopped moving. Stephi hit a key, and a palette of colors appeared in a tiny window at the top of the screen. "Now I'll enhance the picture by adding pixels of color to the stopped frame," she said. She used the mouse to click on different colors and move them down into the picture.

Soon the two dim lines transformed into something more solid. "It looks like a road," Callie said.

Stephi let go of the mouse and sighed. "No, it's too small for a road. It's Gipfel's sewer line."

"Don't we have to do magnetometry tests to be sure?" Frank asked.

Stephi glared at Frank. "You think you know so much about archaeology? Go ahead, waste your time. But I'm telling you now—it's Gipfel's sewer."

Before Frank could reply, Joe stepped into the room, a stack of photos in his hand.

"You're back," Callie said. "You should've seen what the pilot had to go through to get you those photos. We were worried he didn't make it back to Stuttgart."

Joe grinned as he dropped the photos on the desk. "I was the pilot," he said.

"No way!" Callie gasped.

"It was quite an adventure, but I'll fill you in later." He looked around the room. "Don't you have a computer scanner?"

Stephi pointed under the desk. "It's hooked up. We just like to keep it out of the way."

Joe lifted the microwave-size scanner onto the desk and turned it on. In less than ten minutes Frank and Stephi had fed all the photos into the scanner, digitized the information, and uploaded it into Dr. Maxwell's Geographical Information Systems program. Perfect replicas of the photos appeared on the computer screen.

The near infrared film showed the amount of heat reflecting off the ground and made everything look like the surface of the moon. The earth appeared in different shades of gray and looked barren, distorted, as if the pictures had been taken from outer space.

"Let's test my theory and take a look at Zimmermann's property first," Stephi said, clicking through a series of photos. She stopped on one of the photos, staring in disbelief. "Oh, no! Look at these hot spots."

"Fresh soil," Frank said grimly.

Joe peered at the screen. "What?"

"The city council banned Zimmermann from doing anything with his site until we had a chance to prospect it," Stephi said. "But it looks as though he's already bulldozed off the top layer of soil."

"That means if the fort's under there, he could ruin it," Callie said.

"I think I see something else." Using the mouse again, Stephi clicked on one small section of the photograph and enlarged it. She enlarged an even smaller section, and then one even smaller.

A pattern of hazy lines filled the screen.

"It looks like rooms," Frank said. "A hallway here, and over here a thick outside wall."

"Zimmermann isn't about to ruin anything," Stephi said. "He's found the fort, and he's getting ready to excavate it."

Chapter
7

CALLIE'S EYES WENT WIDE. "Are you sure?"

"It's obvious," Stephi said. "From the looks of that photo, these structures are just under some loosely packed soil. I'd say less than six inches."

Frank leaned in close to the screen. "That means Zimmermann could have already uncovered the fort and is just keeping loose dirt on it for secrecy."

"What are these blobs?" Joe asked, pointing to a series of white splotches.

"He must be using heaters to warm the soil," Frank said. "So he can dig."

Joe started for the door. "We've got to confront this guy."

"No." Stephi stood up quickly, almost knocking her chair over. "I mean, it's New Year's Day," she said, trying to keep calm. "Zimmermann won't be in his office. And besides, it'll be dark soon."

Joe had his hand on the doorknob. "We can't just wait around."

"Maybe we should call the police," Callie suggested.

"No," the other three said in unison.

Frank raised his hand to quiet everyone. "I think Stephi's right. Before we go jumping all over Zimmermann, let's do some more work on these pictures."

Stephi sat back down at the computer. "I can overlay relief maps of the area, and I can enhance these photos. Give me a couple of hours. Then we'll know the exact layout of the fort."

"Joe," Frank said, "why don't you and Callie get something to eat while I help Stephi?"

"No, that's all right," Stephi said. "I'd rather work on this myself, if you don't mind."

"You sure?"

"Yeah. I'm still a little upset about Dr. Maxwell not being here. It'll make me feel better to concentrate on this alone."

Frank nodded. "Sure." He followed Joe and Callie down the stairs and out of the carriage house.

"I don't like waiting around," Joe said. "But I have to admit I could use some dinner."

"You should be hungry," Callie teased. "Driving fast cars and doing crazy airplane stunts takes a lot of energy."

Frank grabbed Joe by the shoulder and motioned for Callie to stay quiet. They were by the fountain between the carriage house and the mansion. The sun had just dropped behind the mountain, and the lighted windows of the main house shone brightly in the dark.

Frank didn't see anyone else around. "I want to check something out while Stephi's inside." Going over to the van, he carefully opened the rear door and climbed in. Joe and Callie followed.

Frank found the box with the plastic cylinders. He dug one out and shone his pocket flashlight on it.

"What is it?" Joe asked.

Frank turned the cylinder over. Like the electrodes, it had contact points at one end. "I think it's a fluxgate gradiometer."

Callie suppressed a giggle. "Only you could say words like that with a straight face, Frank."

"Thanks, I think." Frank handed the object to Joe. "Using a fluxgate gradiometer is one of several ways to get magnetic readings from under the soil." He produced the metallic strip from his pocket. "I wasn't sure what it was until I got a close look at it, but it makes sense."

"It isn't making sense to me," Joe said.

"There should be two strips like this inside," Frank said. "They're encased in a quartz tube."

Joe handed the gradiometer to Callie. "So what I found under the van this morning wasn't glass."

"Shattered quartz crystals," Frank said. "When you drive an alternating electrical current through these two metal strips, they measure the magnetic fields in the soil."

"That means Dr. Maxwell must have been out taking magnetic readings last night," Joe said.

"But was he at Gipfel's or Zimmermann's?" Callie asked. "Remember, he had the same pictures and readings we've got."

"We'll check back with Stephi later," Frank said, stepping out of the van. "Maybe she'll see something on the computer that can tell us which site has more promise. And that could lead us to Maxwell—where he's been . . ."

"Or where he is now," Joe finished, reading his brother's thoughts.

"So are you suggesting," Callie said, "that Dr. Maxwell didn't leave the country after all?"

"Well, let's just say that's another part of this mystery that has to be dug up."

Herr von Kubiza didn't come down to dinner, sending word with Gabi that he didn't feel well.

"I told my father that this whole thing was silly," Gabi said. "It is a stupid legend and a waste of time and money."

"I suppose both would be better spent on you,

right?" Joe mumbled, taking a bite of spicy sausage and cabbage.

Gabi scowled at Joe. "It seems Dr. Maxwell agrees with me. Why else would he leave?"

The Hardys and Callie didn't respond.

Gabi stood and tossed her napkin on the table. She put on her leather jacket and pulled a black lipstick from the pocket. "You should all go out with me tonight," she said, applying the makeup. "I'm going to see a great band."

"No, thanks," Frank said.

"Maybe another night," Callie said in an attempt to be friendly.

Gabi left and Joe pushed his plate away. "Should we go check on Stephi?"

"In a minute," Frank said. "I've got an idea."

A moment later they were in Frank's room. He talked as he unpacked his laptop computer and set it up on the nightstand by his bed. "Joe," he said, "if you found the lost shield of Emperor Decius, what would you do with it?"

Joe shrugged. "You know what you're supposed to do with artifacts," he said. "Or do I have to remind you of the lecture you got at customs about smuggling antiquities?"

"What if you needed money?" Frank prodded.

Callie interrupted. "I'd sell it on the black market. But finding a buyer might be hard."

Frank lifted the edge of the comforter and reached under the bed to the phone jack. He unplugged the phone and hooked up the computer modem. Sitting on the bed, he took the computer onto his lap and said, "You could try to find a buyer on the Internet."

"It's fast and cheap," Joe agreed.

"And anonymous, if you're careful," Callie added.

Vanessa Bender's mother, Andrea, owned a computer-animation studio back in Bayport. That would be the safest route to go, Frank figured. "I'm dialing into the server at Mrs. Bender's studio."

Once into the main server, Frank used Telnet to get to the World Wide Web. He did a quick key-word search and landed in a new group focusing on Roman history and artifacts. Next he posted a message to ALL COLLECTORS. It read, "Looking to expand collection of artifacts from the time of Emperor Decius, AD 249–251. Money no object. Decius's shield of particular interest. Contact through this Web site as soon as possible."

"What do you think?"

Joe gave the okay sign. "If Zimmermann or anyone else finds the fort before us, this may lead us right to them."

"I know it's a long shot," Frank said. "But we need to cover all our bases."

Callie looked at her watch. "I wonder how Stephi's doing?"

"Good question," Joe said.

The three teenagers headed downstairs and out the back of the mansion.

"Hey, the van's gone," Joe said, but Frank was already sprinting past him into the carriage house.

Frank burst into the research room. Empty. He clicked through the photos on the computer. "She's gone," he said as Joe and Callie pounded up the steps. "And she didn't do anything to enhance the pictures."

"Did she go to Zimmermann's?" Callie asked.

"Let's find out." Joe said, pulling the keys to the Porsche from his pocket.

The village of Köbingen lay spread out in a wide valley between the mountains. Driving through town, Joe could see the dark water of the Neckar River on his right and brightly lit shops on his left. The buildings were quaint, mostly old houses and Swiss-style ski chalets converted to small groceries, antique stores, and cafés.

Joe checked the rearview mirror again. "I think someone's following us."

Frank fought the impulse to turn in his seat and look back. "What kind of car?" he asked.

"I can't tell. The glare from the headlights is too bright."

Joe cranked the wheel of the Porsche to the left, steering them away from the river and into the maze of narrow village streets. "He's still with us. It might be a dark-colored sedan."

Joe sped up, weaving the 911 through the cobblestone streets. The tires squealed at a traffic circle surrounding some sort of stone and bronze monument. Joe veered off to the right.

"We're going through a park," Callie said.

"I don't see them anymore," Joe said, checking the mirror and slowing down. "Maybe I'm just being paranoid." They passed young couples sitting together on benches. Then an old man walking a dog. When Joe was certain they weren't being tailed, he headed south out of town.

The Zimmermann development was on a flat, wooded plateau high over the river. Joe cut the lights and the engine as they approached, coasting to a stop along a dirt access road.

"There's the van," Frank said, getting out of the Porsche. The white van looked ghostly sitting under some trees ahead of them, abandoned in the dark.

A few yards past the van, the woods ended, and a huge clearing the size of several football fields stretched out under the stars. An eight-foot chain-link fence provided security.

"A perfect place for a fort," Joe whispered. The yellow bulldozers and backhoes he'd seen from the plane were parked at the near end of the compound.

They stayed low as they skirted along the fence, looking for a gate. Joe spotted something ahead and stopped. He whispered over his shoulder to the others, "It looks like one of the crates of equipment from the van."

"It is," Frank said, padding over and lifting the lid. "Stephi must have been planning to do some magnetometry tests after all."

Only a few feet farther on, Joe found the gate. A heavy chain dangled through the latch, and an open padlock lay on the ground. "Stephi must have a key to this place."

"I don't like the looks of this," Frank said. "If she opened the gate, how come she left the box out here?"

"Why don't we ask her?" Joe gently lifted the latch and pulled the gate open. Before Frank could protest, he'd slipped through and disappeared into the darkness.

"Stay here, Callie," Frank said.

"No way, buddy."

Frank could see from her eyes how serious Callie was. "Okay," he said. "Watch our backs."

Frank took a few steps into the darkness and then stopped, listening intently. He thought he heard the sound of someone digging the blade of a shovel into the cold earth.

"Joe," he whispered as loud as he dared. No answer. He clicked on his pocket flashlight, but its narrow beam barely made a difference. Joe was probably moving ahead at his usual breakneck speed, he figured.

Frank could feel Callie behind him as they

walked in the direction of the cliff. The only light came from the stars and the glow of Köbingen far down in the valley. He was pretty sure they were heading toward the fort. He closed his eyes and tried to imagine the photo on the computer screen. Where had the fort been? More to the left? Closer to the cliff? He opened his eyes when he felt Callie's hand on his shoulder.

Suddenly Frank heard a rumble and felt the ground move under his feet. Two bright lights out of nowhere snapped on, blinding him, and the clamor of a large engine rang in his ears.

The light came toward him, growing fast. Callie screamed, and Frank saw a shadow hovering over the lights. It looked like an enormous clawed hand reaching for him out of the darkness.

Chapter

8

FRANK GRABBED CALLIE and dived to his right. They hit the ground hard as the massive shovel of a backhoe slammed into the earth behind them. Frank scrambled to his feet, telling Callie to stay down. The backhoe engine revved, and the jointed hydraulic arm lifted the shovel high overhead and turned it toward them. The steel teeth along the lip of the shovel raked through the air as the arm came down again.

Then, grabbing Callie's arm to help her up, Frank yelled, "We have to split up. Run as fast as you can!"

The shovel smashed between them, its teeth sinking deep into the frozen soil.

Frank was suddenly blinded by the backhoe

lights. It had turned to come after him. He shaded his eyes, trying to see the driver. Then he saw the silhouette of a figure come running out of the darkness. The person disappeared behind the lights.

Frank dived and rolled again as the backhoe thundered past. He realized it was Joe he had seen—he had climbed up into the cab, struggling with the driver.

Frank took off after them. The backhoe was out of control now, and it jolted and bucked over the rutted earth, picking up speed as it headed toward the fence.

Running as fast as he could, Frank caught up to the machine and grabbed for one of the steps coming down from the cab. If he fell, he'd be crushed flat by the huge rear tire.

He looked up just in time to see one of the struggling figures kick the other in the chest. Frank had the lowest step and was reaching for the next when someone tumbled from the cab. The person hit the ground behind him with a heavy thud.

The backhoe was only a few yards from the fence, and as Frank made a final effort to pull himself up, his hand slipped from the cold metal. The rear tire caught his left shoulder. He went down.

Frank felt the air go out of his lungs as he landed on his back. He waited for the backhoe to run over him, knowing he could do nothing to prevent it. But it didn't. It missed him by a fraction of an inch, then crashed through the fence and rumbled down the access road.

"Frank, are you okay?"

Frank rolled over and saw Joe standing over him. "Yeah," he said, managing only a hoarse whisper. "Got the wind knocked out of me."

"We both fell pretty hard." Joe helped his brother up. "That guy was as strong as an ox," he said, rubbing his chest where he'd been kicked. "I thought you were going to get pancaked by that thing."

"So did I."

Callie appeared out of the darkness, her face streaked with dirt. "I found Stephi. She's hurt, but I don't know how badly."

The Hardys followed Callie back toward the cliff. They found Stephi sitting up, holding a blood-soaked handkerchief to her forehead.

"How do you feel?" Frank asked, kneeling beside her.

Stephi stifled a sob. "I think I'm okay. A little dizzy, that's all." She looked up at the others. "I'm sorry," she said. "I just couldn't wait. I was too excited about finding the fort."

"We're going to get you to a doctor," Frank said, helping Stephi to her feet. "The fort can wait until daylight."

Frank and Callie helped Stephi walk to the road while Joe ran ahead to get the van. Then they headed back to Köbingen, Frank driving the girls in the van, while Joe followed in the Porsche.

About halfway back down the access road, Frank spotted the backhoe parked under some trees. Its lights were off and the cab was empty.

Frank glanced over his shoulder. Stephi lay across the backseat of the van under a blanket, her eyes closed.

"Did she tell you what happened?" he asked Callie.

"She said she remembers climbing over the fence. Then she was walking toward the cliff and someone came out of nowhere and demanded to know what she was doing there."

"In German or English?"

"She didn't say. She thought it was a guard. He must have hit her with a flashlight or a tire iron or something, because that's the last thing she remembers."

Frank found the hospital near the center of town and quickly pulled up to the emergency entrance. Inside, several efficient nurses took over, wheeling Stephi into an exam room and ushering the Hardys and Callie into a brightly lit waiting area.

Joe found a vending machine and bought three cups of hot cocoa. "This will help us warm up," he said, sitting down next to Frank and Callie.

Callie's hands shook as she sipped her cocoa. "Stephi gets knocked unconscious. We get chased by a giant bulldozer thing . . . that guard sure had an extreme way of telling us to stay off Zimmermann's property."

Frank used his cup to warm his hands. "If you were guarding a Roman fort filled with priceless artifacts, wouldn't you do anything to keep people away?"

"Guards don't wear ski masks," Joe said. "And why would he take off on a backhoe instead of asking us questions or calling the cops? I think it was the guy who followed us through town."

"But how do you explain the padlock at the gate?" Frank asked. "Whoever attacked us used a key to get in there."

"I don't know," Joe said. "We'll let Zimmermann try to explain tomorrow."

After about a half hour a woman finally stepped into the waiting room and introduced herself as Dr. Walter. She was almost as tall as Joe and wore her brown hair in a tight braid down her back.

"I'm the patient's neurologist," Dr. Walter said. "Your friend has quite a bad bump on her head. She should be okay, but we want to keep her overnight for observation."

"Can we talk to her?" Callie asked.

"She's sleeping now. Why don't you come back early in the morning."

Frank woke the next morning and looked at his alarm clock—5:00 A.M., still dark outside. He'd been restless all night thinking about the fort and Dr. Maxwell. It had been more than twenty-four hours since the archaeologist had disappeared, which meant it was time the police filed the missing-persons report. Maybe it would also be the day the fort was uncovered on Zimmermann's land. If Dr. Maxwell really was hoping to avoid professional embarrassment, the discovery of the fort would vindicate him and bring him out of hiding. At least Frank hoped that was the case.

Frank opened his laptop computer and clicked it on. First he checked his E-mail account. He'd received a brief letter from his father:

Frank and Joe,

I talked to Dr. Maxwell's family. They haven't heard from him. His sudden disappearance seems very unusual to me. See what you can dig up. I'll do what I can from this end.

After exiting his online account, Frank jumped on the Internet and checked the Roman newsgroup. He found no response to the posting he'd entered the day before.

There was a knock at his door, and Joe's head appeared. He hadn't combed his hair yet, and it shot out in all directions. "You up, too?"

"Yup," Frank replied. "No good news. Dr. Maxwell hasn't contacted his family, and no one bit on our Decius artifacts bait."

"Give it time. Get dressed and let's get some breakfast."

The Hardys found Herr von Kubiza down in the breakfast room. He jumped up from the table when they came in.

"Ah, you startled me," he said. "You are up very early this morning." Herr von Kubiza looked even more tired than Frank felt. His hair was slicked back as though he'd just taken a shower, and he wore a white dress shirt and black woolen pants held up with suspenders, but the dark circles under his eyes belied his crisp appearance.

Joe stretched his arms over his head. "Too much going on to sleep late."

"Sit and I will get you something to eat."

"Where's Karl?" Frank asked.

"Oh, it is too early for Karl yet." Herr von Kubiza went to the refrigerator and rummaged around, pulling out a box of orange juice and some bread and fruit.

"We went to check out Herr Zimmermann's land last night," Frank said. "Someone attacked Stephi."

Herr von Kubiza stood up straight, holding the juice in one hand. He twisted his mustache with the other in concern. "Is she all right?"

"We think so," Joe said, sitting down. "She spent the night at the hospital just to be safe."

"This is terrible. I want you to call off the search for the fort. Gabi was right. It's only a silly dream of mine, and now Dr. Maxwell has suffered professional shame and Stephi has been hurt by that greedy Zimmermann."

"How can you give up so easily?" Joe asked. "I think we've found something."

"No, there is nothing," von Kubiza said firmly. He placed the food and some glasses on the table, then motioned for Frank to sit down. "The same thing happened to me in Turkey five years ago."

Frank raised his eyebrows.

"It is true," von Kubiza said. "We were sure our research was correct. But when we went to excavate—nothing. I came back empty-handed."

"We just have a few more things to look at," Frank said.

"Take your short time left here to enjoy Germany. That is what you should do. I am just an old fool."

Frank turned to Joe. "I'm going to go over to the carriage house for a minute to start the GIS programs on our data from yesterday."

"Have something to eat," von Kubiza said. "Some juice at least."

Frank zipped up his parka. "Be right back."

Outside, the sky was purple from the rising sun, and there was just enough light for Frank to see his breath condense in the cold winter air.

He still had Stephi's keys from the night before. But when he started to insert the key into the carriage house door, the door swung open, completely silent on its hinges.

Moving as noiselessly as a cat burglar, Frank

padded into the research center. He went over to Stephi's desk, beneath the picture of the shield, and sifted through the papers there. Nothing was missing.

As he moved to the stairs, he heard an electric whirring noise. Someone was upstairs. Frank slowly ascended, one stair at a time, watching as first the overhead light fixture and then the tops of the filing cabinets came into view over the last step.

He head the whirring again, followed by what sounded like razor blades tearing through cloth.

Reaching the top of the staircase, Frank saw a tall, broad-shouldered person standing by the computer desk. He was dressed entirely in black, with a ski mask covering his face, and heavy combat boots. He was feeding the aerial photographs and the electrical resistivity data into a portable paper shredder.

"Hey!" Frank yelled.

The figure spun to face Frank. He fumbled to grab some computer disks off the desk and then rushed forward, faking left, then going right in an effort to get past Frank to the stairs.

Frank crouched low like a linebacker and drove his shoulder into the man's rib cage. They both went down.

Frank grabbed for the ski mask, trying to rip it off. "Who are you?" he demanded.

The intruder swung wildly. Frank felt his head snap back as the man's fist caught him under the jaw. Tiny dark spots swirled in Frank's eyes as he fought to keep them open. He shook his head, clearing the cobwebs, and lunged again for the mask.

But the trespasser slipped from his grasp and scrambled to the stairs. A computer disk and something that looked like a clod of dirt fell from the man's pocket and skittered across the floor, but Frank had no time to pick them up. He took the stairs two at a time on his way down.

Joe was coming out of the mansion when he saw Frank and the intruder burst from the carriage house. He immediately sprinted the few steps to the driveway, blocking that route of escape.

The masked figure stopped in his tracks for a split second, then ran for the back door of the mansion, disappearing inside.

"Go around to the front!" Frank shouted. "We'll have him trapped."

Frank dashed into the house, through the breakfast room—past an astonished Herr von Kubiza—toward the front of the house.

Frank reached the huge, marble-floored entrance hall and stopped in his tracks. The trespasser had grabbed one of the double-bladed battle-axes from the suit of armor by the front door. Frank got into attack stance as the man came toward him, slashing the deadly blade through the air.

Chapter

9

AS THE MAN MOVED CLOSER, Frank could see the red rims of his eyes behind the ski mask. Frank circled right, trying to get the intruder to turn his back to the front door He knew his brother was behind the door, ready to do his part.

Herr von Kubiza's voice boomed out from the hallway. "What is this?" he yelled.

"Stay back," Frank said.

The attacker lunged at Frank, who ducked and heard the blade whistle over his head. He stepped in low and slammed a right hook into the man's ribs.

The man doubled over but recovered in a split second and swung the ax handle. Frank staggered back as it hit him in the head. He could feel blood trickling down his temple.

The intruder's back now faced the front door, and Frank saw Joe creeping in silently. Frank feinted at the man, then jumped back as the heavy ax cut an arc through the air inches from his chest.

Joe was only a few meters behind the man when his hiking boot squeaked on the slick floor. Whirling instantly, the attacker threw the ax at Joe. Frank saw it flash, end over end, toward his brother. Joe stepped neatly to the side. The ax flew past, hit the front door, and stuck there, its handle quivering.

"Grab him!" Joe yelled.

But the man had already sprinted to the far wall. The mural on the wall showed a scene of Saint Gregor slaying a dragon, and the trespasser opened a door cut into the wall under the dragon and vanished.

Frank turned to von Kubiza. "Where does that door lead?"

"To the basement," von Kubiza managed to say. The man seemed to be stunned by the events he'd witnessed.

At the door, pocket flashlight in hand, Joe said, "I'm going after him."

"It's like a maze down there. We should call the police," Herr von Kubiza said.

"Call them," Frank said as he followed Joe down the narrow, wooden staircase.

The stone basement was cold, musty, and poorly lit by naked bulbs. Joe put his flashlight away—he wanted to have both hands free, just in case.

"Stick together," Frank said.

Joe nodded. The first room was empty, except for an old workbench along one wall. "Herr von Kubiza was right," Joe said as he bent down to pass through a low doorway. "There must be twenty little storage rooms down here."

The next room was obviously the wine cellar. Hundreds of dusty bottles were stacked in wooden racks. "No one here," Joe whispered.

"This way, Joe," Frank called.

Joe turned down a hall and found Frank standing in a room with a huge, ancient, coal-burning furnace. Frank motioned to a short flight of stone steps. "They lead outside," he said. "And the door's open."

Joe looked up the steps. He could see the tops of some trees and the sky. "What is this?" he asked.

"The coal cellar," Frank replied. "When this old furnace was used, you'd open that door up there and just shovel all the coal down in here. Then you had to feed the furnace every few hours."

"So our man in black took off through here."

"Looks that way. He's long gone."

Joe reached up and pulled the steel coal-cellar door shut. "Pretty strange how he knew where to go to escape."

"Maybe he got lucky," Frank said. "But somehow I doubt it."

As they retraced their steps, Joe noticed some crates stacked under the workbench. The words on the milk-crate-size boxes were in German, but Joe immediately recognized the symbol for explosives.

"Frank, over here."

Joe pulled one of the crates out and pried open the lid. After removing several layers of paper and foam backing, he revealed a box of electronic detonators and a flat insert with different geometrical shapes cut out of it. Each of the molded cutouts was filled with a dense, puttylike substance.

"Shaped charges," Frank said.

"Exactly. But what for?"

"Dr. Maxwell wanted them," Herr von Kubiza said, coming down the basement steps. "Did our perpetrator escape?"

"Out the cellar door," Frank said. "I've never heard of using explosives on an archaeological dig."

"The fort has been buried for almost two thousand years," von Kubiza said, stooping to pick up the lid to the crate. "Dr. Maxwell figured trees would have grown over it, or perhaps boulders from the mountainside might have fallen on it. We thought we might need the explosives to clear the land for the excavation."

"Shaped charges would allow you to direct the

explosive in just the direction you wanted," Frank said. "I guess that makes sense."

"Yes," Herr von Kubiza said. "We wanted to be prepared for anything. But how could we be prepared for poor Dr. Maxwell going crazy?"

"What do you mean?" Joe asked.

"Who else could it be?" von Kubiza said. "I checked the carriage house. Whoever the intruder was shredded all the photos and data you got to replace what I brought back from the university on New Year's Eve."

"And the carriage house wasn't broken into," Frank said. "The door was open when I went over there."

Herr von Kubiza started back up the stairs. "Dr. Maxwell and Stephi have the only keys to the carriage house," he said. "Come. The police are on the way, and I don't wish to have to explain these explosives in my basement."

When they got upstairs, the police were pulling into the driveway, sirens blaring. Gabi and Callie stood in the entrance hall looking sleepy and confused.

"What is all this terrible racket?" Gabi demanded. "I need to sleep."

"Someone tried to practice his lumberjack skills on us," Joe said, gesturing to the ax in the door.

This information didn't seem to faze Gabi at all. "It is Zimmermann's men pestering us some more. Now that we know the fort is a myth, we should let him go ahead with his construction. That's what I think."

"This guy did more than just *pester* us," Joe said. Before he could add anything more, the police arrived, and the Hardys spent the next hour going over their story. The detective in charge promised to start the missing-persons paperwork on Dr. Maxwell along with the robbery report. A uniformed officer spent a long time meticulously labeling a pile of evidence bags containing shredded bits of paper and photographs he'd collected from inside the carriage house.

"Those officers seemed nice and thorough," Joe said after they'd left. He couldn't hide the sarcasm in his voice. "It'll be summer before they turn anything up."

Herr von Kubiza frowned. "Köbingen is a small town. They are not used to this much excitement, but I am sure they will find Dr. Maxwell if we let them do their job." He went to a closet and pulled out a heavy overcoat. "I must get to the university. Call me if you hear any news."

Back in the kitchen the Hardys found Callie ready to go to the hospital to visit Stephi. Gabi, apparently, had gone back to bed. Frank gave Callie the van keys and kissed her on the cheek. "Be careful," he said. "This is starting to get serious."

Callie looked worried. "You don't really think the attacker was Dr. Maxwell, do you?"

"No, not unless Dad is totally mistaken about the character of his old roommate."

"That guy seemed a bit too athletic for an eccentric scientist," Joe said, taking a bite out of an apple. "But I could be underestimating him."

Frank and Joe walked Callie to the van. "Like I said," Frank told Callie, "I want you to be careful. I'm not convinced Stephi doesn't have something to do with Dr. Maxwell's disappearance, so watch yourself."

"You, too," Callie said, waving as she drove off.

The Hardys hurried to the carriage house. "I'm going to start this computer enhancement before we go visit our friend Herr Zimmermann," Frank said, sitting down at the desk upstairs.

"I want to see how you do this." Joe stood behind his brother, watching him tap at the keyboard and use the mouse to click quickly through different files and programs.

Frank worked for a few minutes, then leaned back in the chair, a scowl on his face. He scratched his head and opened a few more files, then seemed to give up.

"What's wrong?" Joe asked.

"The masked man did more than shred a few documents," Frank said. "The photos and stuff are still on the hard drive, but Dr. Maxwell's GIS programs are a total mess."

"Can you fix them?"

"We don't have time for that." Frank slapped

the side of the monitor so hard it almost toppled off the desk. "We'll just have to do without them."

Joe had rarely seen his brother so frustrated. Usually he was as cool as a snowboarder on a long mountain run. "What about Vanessa?"

"What about Vanessa?" Frank snapped.

"Why don't we zap the data to Bayport and let her work on it?"

Frank smiled. "I thought you didn't know anything about computers."

"Think again, bro," Joe said.

Frank sat down again, programmed Vanessa's number into the modem, and started sending files. After he'd sent all the digitalized photos and the resistivity readings they'd taken on Herr Gipfel's property, he fed in some topographical surveys and satellite images. Including a long letter of instructions on what they needed, the whole process took over an hour. The computer was still buzzing away when Frank stood and stretched.

A stray computer disk lying on top of the printer caught Frank's attention. "Hey, I just remembered something," he said.

Joe watched as his brother got down on his hands and knees and started crawling around the floor. "What are you looking for?"

"A disk and something else fell out of that guy's pocket while we were fighting," Frank said. He reached under the desk and produced the computer disk. He read the label and tossed the disk aside. "Nothing important now that Vanessa has all the data," he said.

"Is this it?" Joe handed Frank the clod of dirt. It was about the size of a golf ball and was very solid and heavy. "I found it behind the door."

"Yeah," Frank said. "Let's see what we have here." He dug around in some cardboard boxes. "Find me a glass jar or something."

Joe found a big coffee mug on Stephi's desk downstairs and brought it up. "Will this work?"

Frank nodded. "Uh-huh." He placed the ball of dirt in the mug and poured something from a plastic bottle over it. He saw his brother's quizzical expression and explained, "It's acid."

The acid bubbled up around the clod, and within seconds the whole concoction was a muddy, boiling mess. Frank waited a few minutes, then cautiously carried the mug to the sink in Dr. Maxwell's room. He had already filled the sink with water.

Joe watched as Frank slowly poured the acid into the sink. The glob of dirt stayed behind, stuck to the bottom of the mug. Frank had to reach in, using the tail of his shirt to keep from getting burned, and pull the thing out.

They went back to the research room, where Frank picked a wire brush from one of the boxes and began to scrub away at what became a flat disk.

"I don't believe it," Joe said.

"Believe it."

The ball of dirt was now a gold disk, tarnished and dirty. "It's a Roman coin," Joe said, taking it from Frank.

"This proves Herr Gipfel was right," Frank said. "Someone has already found the treasure."

"Yeah, but who?" Joe asked, holding the coin up to the light. "Maxwell or Zimmermann?"

Chapter

10

"I THINK WE HAVE all the evidence we need to
confront Zimmermann," Frank said, his jaw set.
"Let's see what he has to say."

Frank drove the Porsche this time as they
wound back down the twisting mountain road
and into town.

The Zimmermann Construction headquarters
was a building six stories tall and cylindrical in
shape, like a storage tank at an oil refinery. The
entire building was covered with mirrored glass
and shiny black tile. Even the sign in front of the
building was silver and black.

They pulled into the parking lot, and Frank got
out and looked up at the sky. The morning had
turned dark and overcast. He hoped it would

snow. If it snowed, he figured, excavating the fort would become even more difficult, and that would give them more time.

Joe reached the front door and beckoned for Frank to follow. Inside, they were greeted immediately by a severe-looking, silver-haired receptionist.

"We're here to see Herr Zimmermann," Frank said in English.

The receptionist opened a black date book and ran her finger down a list of names. "Do you have an appointment?"

"No, but it's regarding his development property south of town. It's very important."

"I'm sorry, but without an—"

Joe interrupted. "We work for Herr von Kubiza."

"Ah, I see," the receptionist said. "That is different. One moment." She turned and spoke quietly in German into her intercom.

Joe smiled. "See, Frank, you just needed to know the password."

At that moment the chrome doors of an elevator opened, and two men in dark blue business suits stepped out. They were each at least six-foot-four. One's head was completely shaved, and the other wore his hair in a flattop.

Joe suddenly felt unwelcome. "I don't think they're here to escort us to Zimmermann," he said under his breath.

"No, we are not," one of the men said curtly. "We are here to show you to your car."

Joe bristled and got right in the man's face. "We're here to see the boss, not you two bums."

"Easy, Joe," Frank said, putting his hand on his brother's shoulder. "This isn't the time or place to start something."

Frank almost had to drag Joe from the building. As long as the two security guards watched them from the front door, Frank kept walking toward the car. But when he saw them disappear back inside, he nudged Joe with his elbow. "Come on. Maybe there's another way in."

The Hardys left the parking lot and walked around the block, hoping to spot a rear entrance to the structure. "It's hard to sneak up on a round building made of glass," Joe said.

"This way, Joe." Frank cut between two trees and pointed. The back parking lot was filled with trucks and construction equipment. "The trucks will give us cover until we get close."

The trucks all carried the same crane design that they'd seen on the side of the rig that had chased them on the autobahn. Frank and Joe stayed low as they crossed the lot. They stopped and crouched behind the rear tires of one of the trucks when they got close to the building.

"That looks like a service entrance," Frank said, pointing to a pair of black steel double doors.

Joe started for the doors, but his brother

stopped him. "Hold on," Frank said. "Here comes our ticket in."

A silver van pulled into the lot and slowly drove past them. As it went by, the Hardys jogged from their hiding place and tailed the van to the doors, being careful to stay in the driver's blind spot so he couldn't see them in his side mirrors.

A man wearing a hard hat jumped from the van, unlocked the doors, and went in. Joe scrambled for the doorknob but got there too late. The door slammed shut.

Joe took a credit card from his wallet and tried to slide it between the doors. "No good," he muttered when the card bent in half. He then tried his lock pick, working the wires into place.

"This is taking too long," Frank whispered.

"I've almost got it. One more turn and . . . oh, man."

"What?"

"This place is like a fortress. The lock chewed up my pick and didn't even budge." Joe heard voices coming from behind the door. "Somebody's coming," he hissed.

The Hardys sprinted from the lot. When they were safely behind the row of trucks, they turned back to see the man in the hard hat come out of the door with the other men, climb into the van, and drive off.

"Back to the car," Frank said. "We'll find Zimmermann's home address at the mansion and track him down tonight."

Both the van and Gabi's hatchback were in the driveway when Frank and Joe returned to Herr von Kubiza's.

"See if you can find an address for Zimmermann," Frank said as they went in the back door. "I'm going upstairs to check in on the Internet."

Joe wandered around the first floor. The place seemed to be deserted. He checked the drawers of the antique rolltop desk where the phone was, but didn't see a phone book or list of addresses.

He found Gabi in a back room, lounging on a foldout futon and watching music videos on TV. "Anything good on?" he asked.

"My favorite band, so be quiet."

"I'm looking for Zimmermann's address," Joe persisted.

"My father's office," Gabi said. "Around the corner and down the hall. Now be quiet."

"Thanks." Joe closed the door behind him and headed down the hall.

Herr von Kubiza's office was big and richly decorated. Bookcases lined the walls, and a plush, burgundy-colored carpet covered the floor. A heavy desk sat in front of the only window, facing out to a view of Köbingen down in the valley.

In no time Joe found the phone book and wrote down Zimmermann's listing on a scrap of paper. Then a stack of letters caught his attention. They were postmarked for that morning. He flipped through them, stopping when he noticed the Zimmermann crane insignia on one of the return addresses. Joe stuffed the letter in his coat pocket and went to find Frank.

He took the four flights of stairs three steps at a time. Once he'd paused on the landing to catch his breath, Joe found Frank and Callie in Frank's room, staring at the computer screen. "Any news?"

"Stephi's fine," Callie said. "She's resting in her room. Frank's searching through the Roman newsgroup now."

"Got two messages," Frank said. He read the first one aloud:

" 'I have many Roman artifacts available for private collection or museum. Please contact me at (607) 555–1468 New York, USA, anytime.' "

Joe started to comment, but Frank raised his hand. "Wait. Listen to the second one: 'Emperor Decius—711/3223–22563–0.' "

"Wow! Short and to the point," Joe said.

Frank looked up. "Right. And it's a local number. I think someone took the bait."

"Good going, Frank," Joe said. "I've got something, too." Joe took the letter and address from his pocket and handed them to Frank. "That's a note from Zimmermann—written in German."

Frank scanned the letter. "Zimmermann says that now that Dr. Maxwell claims there is no fort, he's going to petition the city council to lift the construction ban."

"How did he know about Dr. Maxwell so soon?" Callie asked.

Frank put the letter back in its envelope and said, "Good question."

"Ten bucks says it's Gabi," Joe said. "She probably couldn't wait to make a fool of her father in public."

"We'll deal with that later." Frank stored the messages onto the hard drive. "Right now we've got to reel in this fish we caught."

"How're you going to do that?" Callie asked.

Frank smiled. "It isn't how *we're* going to do it, it's how *you're* going to do it."

Callie put her hands on her hips. "You'd better fill me in on what's going on, Frank Hardy."

"How would you like to pose as a rich collector of Roman antiquities?" Frank asked.

Now it was Callie's turn to smile. "Sure, I could do that."

"No way," Joe said. "Too dangerous."

"I can handle myself," Callie fired back. She turned to Frank. "What's your plan?"

"You call the number and set up an appointment. Try to make the meeting in a public place—that'll be safer." Frank went to the dresser and dug around in the top drawer. "Here, take my microcassette recorder and get the conversation on tape."

"What do we do?" Joe asked.

"Callie takes the Porsche, so she'll fit the part of a rich collector, and we'll follow her in the van. Nothing will happen without us watching."

Joe seemed satisfied. "Okay," he said. "But watch yourself. We've already had some close calls around here."

"There's a phone in my room," Callie said. "Let's go." Once in her room, she sat on the bed and put the phone on her lap. She took a few deep breaths, then picked up the receiver and dialed the numbers as Frank read them to her.

She got an answer on the first ring. "Hello," a male voice said.

Callie gave Frank the thumbs-up and held the phone away from her head so he and Joe could hear what the man said. "I believe I received a message from you regarding Emperor Decius. We should talk, but not over the phone."

"I agree," the voice said. "You aren't the police, are you?"

"No, of course not," Callie said.

"Good. Where are you calling from?"

"Köbingen."

"That is very good. There is a public phone outside the Café Struldbrugs. Be there in one hour."

The line went dead.

"Hung up," Callie said. She glanced at her watch. It was just past noon. "Out, out, out. I've got less than an hour to get ready."

When Callie came downstairs forty minutes

later, she looked at least ten years older than her eighteen years. She had her blond hair pulled back tight and wore her cat-eye sunglasses and a thick gold necklace.

"Nice jewelry," Frank said.

"You like it?" Callie asked, twisting the gold around her finger. "Stephi lent it to me."

Frank went over the plan once more as they stepped out to the driveway. "Joe and I will go first in the van," he said. "We'll pull over and park about a block from the café. You drive past us and park by the phone. We'll be watching the whole time."

"Don't worry," Callie said as she gunned the Porsche engine. "It'll go fine." She pulled her sunglasses down her nose and peered over the rims at Frank. "Got any cash on you, honey? I don't think I have enough for an emerald-encrusted shield."

"Real funny," Frank said. He got in the van next to Joe and they took off toward town.

Fifteen minutes later they were staked out in front of a ski shop. They could see Callie sitting in the Porsche less than a hundred meters ahead of them, parked at the curb.

The pay phone on the sidewalk looked like a red egg on a stalk. Even with the gloomy, cold weather, shoppers milled about the sidewalk, stepping in and out of stores. People leaving shops pulled their hats down low against the wind, and those entering unwrapped their scarves as they went in.

Frank had his window rolled down. "Is that the phone ringing?"

Joe listened for a second before he said, "I think so. Look, she's getting out to answer it."

"No, Callie," Frank murmured anxiously. "Stay in the car, stay *in* the car." He wished she could read his thoughts. It was enough that she was nearby the phone. It might draw out their collector so that they could identify the person. Callie was putting herself in unnecessary danger by leaving the car.

He watched her pick up the phone and say something into the receiver. Then a black van pulled in behind the Porsche and blocked his view. "Come on, come on. Get out of the way," Frank said through clenched teeth. He started to get out of the van.

"Easy, Frank," Joe said. "Give it a minute."

A few seconds passed, then the black van finally pulled away. The Porsche was still there, but Callie had vanished.

Chapter

11

"SOMEONE GRABBED CALLIE!" Frank shouted.
"She's in that van!"

"I'm right on them, Frank." Joe swung the
white van into traffic and hit the accelerator.
They lost sight of the other van as it rounded
a corner.

"Don't lose them!" Frank yelled. He had both
fists clenched and was pounding on the dash. "I
can't believe I let her do this."

Joe spotted the van up ahead. "There they are.
You want me to catch up to them or hang back?"

Frank watched the van. The driver didn't seem
to be in any particular hurry. The elder Hardy's
natural cool-headedness started to return. "Give
them a minute or two," he said, his voice on

edge. "We'll see where they're going. If they do anything strange, like turn off these busy streets, then we let them know we're here."

"Got it."

As soon as the van swung off the main road along the Neckar River and went south, Frank knew where they were headed. "We're on our way to Zimmermann Construction," he said.

"We were right! Zimmermann must have found the fort," Joe said.

"And he must have found something he wants to sell—like that gold coin his goon dropped."

"Or a priceless shield," Joe added. "But what's he going to do if he finds out Callie isn't a real buyer?"

Frank watched the van like a hawk. "Whatever it is, better get to his place first so we can stop him."

Though the streets were narrow, Joe pulled out and passed a woman on a scooter. The van was just ahead of Joe, and there was no room to go around it.

"Go this way," Frank said, pointing down a one-way street.

The tires screeched and the white van leaned dangerously as Joe wrenched the wheel to the right. "I hope you know what you're doing," he said to Frank.

"Now go left."

Joe whipped the wheel to the left and hit the brakes, swinging the rear end of the van around.

He mashed the accelerator again and tore down a cobblestone alley. Apartment buildings rose up on both sides of the road. Garbage cans and parked bicycles flashed past.

"Left again."

This time Joe skidded. He fought the wheel, trying to bring the van under control. He thought for sure they were going to plow straight into a building when the van came out of the skid and barreled down the next alley. A tin garbage can bounced off the front fender with a terrific clatter, and trash exploded in every direction.

"Duck down!" Frank shouted as they emerged from the alley in a spray of paper and foam cups.

Joe bent over so his head was barely above the steering wheel. He saw the black van coming down the road, about forty feet away, and pulled smoothly in front of it.

"Think they saw us?" Frank asked.

"No, I think we're all right." Joe continued down the street. He wanted as much distance as possible between them and the van before they all arrived at the Zimmermann building.

Joe parked on the street, near the entrance to the parking lot. When the black van pulled in, the Hardys trotted along behind it. A row of trees hid them from pedestrians on the sidewalk, and they just had to hope no one was watching from behind the mirrored glass of the construction company headquarters.

The van stopped at the rear entrance. It was

the same door Joe had tried but failed to get into earlier in the day. This time Joe was sure his quick reflexes wouldn't let him down.

They heard the side door of the van slide open. German-speaking voices filtered out. Peering around the back of the van, Joe watched as one of the tall guards they'd seen earlier stepped out. He unlocked the steel double door and held it open while the other guard escorted Callie into the building.

The first guard followed them, pulling the door shut behind him. But Joe was ready to pounce. Before the bolt could click into place, he jammed his credit card between the two doors. The card blocked the bolt.

Frank and Joe paused outside the entrance, waiting a few seconds to allow the area inside to clear. Then Joe slowly eased the door open and, staying low, crept in. Frank followed.

They found themselves in some sort of storage area. The walls were bare cement block. Steel shelves packed with tools and supplies rose all the way to the ceiling, and bags of cement stacked on wooden pallets formed a pyramid in the center of the area. A forklift sat idle near the entrance.

Frank pointed to the service elevator. The lights above the doors blinked from 2 to 3. "I'd say they're going all the way up to six," he whispered.

"There have to be stairs someplace, in case of a fire."

"Here." Frank pulled open a steel door a few meters down from the elevator. Together, the Hardys charged up the six flights of cement stairs. Phosphorescent emergency lights buzzed on every landing and cast an eerie purple glow on the cinder-block walls.

The door on the sixth-floor landing was unlocked. Frank opened it just a crack and scanned the area inside. It was office space, lavishly decorated in sharp contrast to the barren stairwell where Frank stood.

Thick, light gray carpeting covered the floor, and all the light fixtures were accented with chrome. The secretary's desk in the center of the room was curved marble—shaped like a crescent moon. A young, slender woman with short brown hair sat at the desk talking on the telephone.

Frank heard the elegant ping of the elevator arriving. Then he saw the two guards come into view. They led Callie past the desk and into an office.

"It's time to make our entrance," Frank said.

As he and Joe walked toward the office door, the secretary jumped up from her chair. The phone slipped from her hand and clattered on the desktop.

"Betret für Unbefugte verboten!"

"Are you going to stop us?" Frank said, going straight up to the office door and yanking it open.

Frank found himself face-to-face with the two guards in business suits. The guard with the flat-top stuck his index finger in Frank's chest and grunted, "How did you get in here?"

"You let us in," Joe said, pushing his way through the door and into the office. A man in a business suit sat at a large conference table, but Joe didn't have time to say hello. Out of the corner of his eye he saw the bald guard cock his arm to throw a punch.

Joe ducked down and stepped toward the man, nailing him in the gut with an elbow. The guard doubled over in pain, and Joe stood up sharply as if heading a soccer ball. There was a loud *pop* as he smashed his forehead into the guy's nose, and the guy buckled to his knees.

This happened so quickly that the first guard still had his finger in Frank's chest. He turned to help his partner fight Joe. At that instant Frank grabbed him by the wrist and pivoted hard, flipping the big man over his shoulder. He hit the floor so hard he bounced.

The two brothers stood over the crumpled guards, ready to knock them out if they tried to stand. Joe loosened his shoulders with a few rolls and cracked his knuckles. "Nice workout they gave us," he said. "I needed to get a few kinks out."

"Yup. Keeps those reflexes sharp, too," Frank said. He turned to Callie and asked her if she was okay.

"I'm fine, Frank." Callie rose from the straight-back chair she'd been sitting in and walked over to Frank. He clasped her hand briefly.

"It looks as though the three of you know each other," a voice said from the end of the oval conference table.

"You must be Herr Zimmermann," Joe said.

A distinguished-looking man around fifty years old stood up from the head of the table. His hair was jet black, fading to gray at the temples, and his expensive dress shoes squeaked as he walked across the carpet.

"Correct," he said primly, placing his hands together in front of his chest. He looked as if he were going to say a prayer. "And the two of you must be the same young men who tried to see me this morning. You work for Herr von Kubiza, yes?"

Frank and Joe stepped over to face Herr Zimmermann. The two guards got to their feet, the bald one pinching his nose to stop the flow of blood. When they moved toward the Hardys, Zimmermann waved them off. "I will talk to them alone," he said.

Frank watched the men leave. "We *were* working for Dr. Maxwell," he said.

"But Dr. Maxwell has run off in disgrace," Zimmermann said with a wry smile.

"Who told you that?" Joe demanded.

Herr Zimmermann picked up a newspaper from the conference table. "It is no secret," he said. "Here, I will translate the headline of our local paper for you." He pulled a pair of reading glasses from his suitcoat pocket and put them on. "It says, 'American Archaeologist Fails—Decius's Shield Only a Myth.'" Zimmermann handed the paper to Frank and folded his spectacles back into his pocket. "The source of the information is anonymous, of course."

Frank glanced at the article, then tossed it on the table. "But you know this isn't true. The fort is on your land."

"No," Callie said, putting her hand on Frank's arm. "I already asked Herr Zimmermann if he had any artifacts to sell."

"And I have already stated that I have nothing of the kind." Herr Zimmermann pulled three chairs out from the table and motioned for the teenagers to sit. "I am afraid there has been a terrible misunderstanding."

Joe hesitated to sit down. He didn't want to get too comfortable with the two thugs right outside the door, though they weren't in top form at the moment. Just in case, he adjusted his chair so he could see if anyone entered.

"Why did you answer our Internet ad?" Frank demanded.

"Because I cannot afford any more delays," Herr Zimmermann said, interlacing his fingers and placing his hands on the table. "My investors and I paid four million deutsche marks for that

111

property—almost two million dollars. We are losing thousands every day."

Frank studied Zimmermann's face for signs that he was lying. "What does that have to do with the ad?"

"Even with the news about Dr. Maxwell, my support on the city council is thin," Herr Zimmermann said. "Thanks to that pompous fool von Kubiza, many people around here continue to believe Decius's shield exists. I just wanted to have a talk with whoever was continuing to spread rumors of this legend."

Joe slapped his hands down flat on the table. "By kidnapping? That makes a lot of sense!"

Zimmermann pursed his lips together. "I would not call it kidnapping, but I admit I used poor judgment."

"It isn't a legend," Frank said. "We have aerial photos of your property. We know you've uncovered the fort."

"What! That is ridiculous." Zimmermann seemed flustered for the first time. He gestured to Callie. "As I told your friend here, I have done a little grading to even out the land, but no digging. I have to show my investors I'm doing *something,* even with the construction ban." Zimmermann's face was red with anger. "And as for your absurd notion about the fort, well, the only thing underground on my land is the foundation of a house that burned down years ago."

Chapter

12

FRANK FELT HIS STOMACH do a flip-flop. He couldn't believe it. How could he have been so wrong about the photographs of Zimmermann's land? He wanted to take the Roman coin out of his pocket and slap it on the table, but he resisted the temptation. Until he found out exactly where the coin came from, he didn't want the cops or anyone he didn't trust, like Zimmermann, asking questions about it.

Joe's voice broke the stunned silence. "If you've got nothing to hide, then why did one of your guards almost decapitate my brother with a backhoe last night?"

"You were there?" Zimmermann asked. He seemed genuinely surprised. "I was told some vandals ruined the fence."

"You didn't have a guard posted?" Callie asked.

Zimmermann shook his head.

"So who else has a key?" Frank asked. "Because the gate was open when we got there."

Zimmermann straightened his tie and stood up. "The only person other than the job foreman was Dr. Maxwell. I sent him a key by messenger New Year's Eve morning."

"No way!" Callie gasped.

Frank remembered the note from Dr. Maxwell, the one with the *T* in *theory* capitalized. Maybe it *was* just a typo. That clue sure seemed to be growing insubstantial compared to all the evidence that was piling up against his father's old friend.

Herr Zimmermann stared out the window, wearing a peeved expression. Frank noticed that the tinted glass made everything outside look a hazy green color, as if they were all in a bubble under the ocean.

Frank rubbed his eyes with the heels of his hands. "Considering the circumstances, then," he said to Zimmermann, "you won't mind if we go check your property for ourselves, right?"

Zimmermann turned to Frank and waved his hand in the air. "Yes," he said with a sigh. "Go ahead. This craziness about the lost fort has to end somewhere." Raising his index finger, he said, "But my men go with you. And once you have seen for yourselves that the fort is not there, I want von Kubiza out of my business immediately."

Joe started to object, but his brother cut him off. "That sounds fair," Frank said.

Half an hour later the three vehicles—the black van, the white van, and the cherry red 911 Turbo—were parked at Zimmermann's development. Four or five construction workers were busy repairing the fence crushed by the backhoe.

"You can't go out into the field in those shoes," Frank said to Callie as he pulled a pickax from the back of the van.

"I'll survive," Callie replied.

"No, stay here." Frank leaned close and whispered, "If something happens, get in the car and go for help."

Callie nodded.

Frank tossed a short-handled shovel to Joe, and they started across the frozen lot with Zimmermann's two men. The bald bodyguard had cotton stuffed in his nose. Joe expected the guards to be angry about the fight earlier, but as they walked toward the cliff, he sensed a grudging respect coming from them.

The guard with the buzz haircut had his hands in the pockets of his overcoat. "What do you plan to do with this treasure, if you find it?" he asked.

"Anything you find on an archaeological dig should go to a museum," Frank replied.

"Ach," the bald man said. "There is no money in that, is there?"

"I guess not," Frank replied.

The bald man raised his fists into a boxing stance and took a playful jab at Joe. "You should think about boxing, yes?" He laughed. "Now, there's good money for you."

"Only if you'll be my sparring partner," Joe said, smiling.

"Oh, no. I don't think so."

"This is it," Frank said. They were less than twenty meters from the edge of the cliff. "It's amazing how much easier it is to get your bearings in the daylight." He took his pickax and swung it into the hard earth. Joe joined him, using the shovel.

The cold wind blowing up from the river whipped their hair around their faces. Joe dug faster to keep warm, putting his whole body behind the shovel. Then he felt a shock run up his arms as his shovel clanked into a hard object. "I've got something!" he said excitedly. He turned the blade of the shovel around backward and used it to scrape away the dirt.

Frank knelt down eagerly, his eyes riveted to the spot. Joe had uncovered a smooth patch of cement. A few inches from the center of the patch was a rusted pipe, leading down into the earth.

"It's a bathtub drain," Frank said, his voice flat and tired. "Zimmermann was telling the truth."

"Ah," the bald man said to his partner. "He will be very pleased, yes?"

Joe threw down his shovel in disgust.

It was late afternoon by the time the Hardys and Callie returned to Herr von Kubiza's mansion. They found Stephi sitting in the library, enjoying a crackling fire and a cup of strong tea.

"How are you feeling?" Callie asked as she flopped down in one of the overstuffed chairs that faced the fire.

"Doing a little better," Stephi said, managing to smile. She touched the swollen bruise on her forehead self-consciously. "Tell me what I've missed."

Joe sank into a soft chair, but Frank remained standing.

"We checked Zimmermann's land," Joe said, finally. "No luck."

Stephi's jaw dropped. "But we saw the photographs. How can that be?"

"We must not have been careful enough," Frank said. "We all wanted to see the fort in those pictures. It turned out to be an old, burned-down house."

Joe grabbed a biscuit off a silver tea tray and took a bite. "Herr Zimmermann thinks it was Dr. Maxwell who attacked you last night."

"That's impossible!" Stephi cried. She winced and touched her head again. "We had disagreements, sure, but they were professional, not personal. Dr. Maxwell would never hurt anyone."

"We don't know what to think," Callie said, pouring Stephi another cup of tea. "Now we're back to square one."

"Did Herr von Kubiza get back from the university?" Frank asked. He wanted to show their host the Roman coin. Von Kubiza would be upset to find out he'd been betrayed by Dr. Maxwell, but at least he'd know the fort was out there somewhere. They just had to find it before Dr. Maxwell—or whoever it was—dug up all the artifacts and sold them on the black market.

"He was here," Stephi said, "but he went out again."

Callie took a sip of tea. "I keep wondering why he has so much work to do at the university over winter break."

"He likes to do research while the students are gone," Stephi said. "It's quieter. He did have something to relay to you guys, though. Herr Gipfel called and left a message on the answering machine, reminding you to go to the Esslingen *Schneefest* tonight. He wants you to get some German culture before you leave."

"I'm hardly in the mood to listen to people yodel right now," Joe muttered.

"Come on," Callie said. "We need a break."

Frank turned to go upstairs. "I want to check something first," he said.

In his bedroom Frank checked his E-mail. He

had a message from Vanessa. She said she was working on the computer enhancement and would have something by around midnight that night, Bayport time—not until early the next morning Frank's time.

There was nothing left Frank could do. "It looks as if Callie gets her wish," he mumbled to himself.

The Porsche was too small to fit four comfortably, so the Hardys, Callie, and Gabi took the train to the nearby town of Esslingen. Stephi said she still didn't feel strong enough to go out.

Esslingen turned out to be a medieval city built on the Neckar River thirty miles upstream from Köbingen. From the train station the teenagers simply followed the crowd to the *Schneefest.* As they walked the cobblestone streets, they could see the city lights reflected on the water. A walled fortress sat atop a mountain on the opposite side of the river.

Soon they reached the bustling market square, which was packed with people of all ages. Strings of colored lights marked paths among the vendors' tables and stands. Thick smells of cinnamon and gingerbread warmed the cold air.

"I think I've reached paradise," Callie said.

"It can't be paradise until you have something to eat," Joe joked. He headed straight to a bin of candied almonds and held out a five-mark coin. The vendor took it and handed him back a paper funnel filled with the sticky-sweet nuts.

"You had better let me help you with those," Gabi said, reaching into the package. She had redyed her hair bright orange with yellow tips. It looked to Joe as if her head were on fire.

Suddenly a rumble of applause poured out of the circus tent at the end of the square. Joe turned and saw dozens of other teenagers headed for the entrance. "What's going on over there?" he asked.

"That is why we are here," Gabi said. "Good music and dancing. Follow me." Gabi led the way through the crowd and up the wooden stairs to the tent platform.

Frank held the canvas door open, and they slipped inside. The tent was at least forty meters long. A stage at the far end was loaded with speakers and amplifiers. The backdrop behind the stage was a panoramic view of a city burning at night. In red letters were the words *Tote Gebäude*.

"What's that mean?" Joe asked.

" 'Dead Buildings,' " Gabi replied. "The tightest, most excellent band ever. They play industrial thrash."

"Let's try to get up front," Joe suggested. They tried to push forward, but it became difficult as they neared the stage.

An unseen announcer said something over the public-address system. It was too fuzzy for Frank to understand, but everyone in the tent raised their hands over their heads and started clapping.

Flames shot up from the stage floor, and the amplified sound of a blowtorch ripped through the air. Then four leather-clad musicians burst onto the stage. The crowd erupted as the band blasted into the first song, blending a pounding beat with distorted sound of machinery and chanting human voices.

Everyone started moshing. A big German kid crashed into Joe's chest, sending him to the floor. But just as quickly as he'd been knocked down, several hands reached out and helped him up. Soon he had the hang of it, crashing his body into the crowd, bouncing around like a human pinball.

"This is great!" Joe yelled, but the music was too loud for anyone to hear.

The band cranked for well over an hour before they took their first break. Frank wiped the sweat off his forehead with a shirtsleeve. His ears buzzed and tingled. He leaned over to Joe. "That was incredible."

"Except that you had to keep helping me off the floor," Callie said, brushing off her jeans.

"That is the whole idea!" Gabi shouted. "You help each other back up."

Frank looked at his watch. "We should probably get going."

"And miss the next set?" Joe said. "No way."

Frank slung his arm around his brother's shoul-

121

der. "We're getting up pretty early tomorrow. Come on."

"I am going to stay," Gabi said. "I will catch the next train."

Callie and the Hardys wove their way out of the tent. The crisp air felt great after an hour and a half inside the tent. Joe pulled his damp shirt from his chest as they walked back through the market square. "I'm glad you accepted the tickets from Gipfel," he said to Frank. "Candied almonds and rock and roll is a cultural combination I can appreciate."

"See, Joe? I knew you'd like it," Frank said. "Pretty soon you'll be wearing lederhosen and dancing to an oompah band."

"What's lederhosen?" Joe said.

"Leather shorts," Callie said. "Usually worn with suspenders."

Joe snorted and muttered, "Probably not my best look."

The train whistle blew as soon as they hit the platform. The teenagers sprinted toward the door and hopped aboard the train just as it began to move. As it pulled away, Frank saw the two men step out from behind a pillar on the platform. He thought he saw them pull ski masks over their faces, but when he looked back, they were gone. The platform was completely empty.

Frank opened the door to the second-class compartment and held it for Callie and Joe. As he stepped in after them, he heard the sliding door between train cars open behind him. A cold wind pushed at his back, and he caught a whiff of oil and cigarettes.

Then Frank felt a hand on his collar. Someone very strong pulled him backward. Losing his balance, Frank reached back and grabbed for the arm. He fell to the floor of the train car, catching a glimpse of two heavyset men in ski masks. Then he felt the toe of a boot strike his ribs, and all the air rushed out of his lungs.

One thug opened the car door, while the other one dragged him across the floor. The cold wind rushed in and made his eyes tear, blurring Frank's vision. But he could still make out the tracks rushing beneath him at fifty miles an hour.

"Auf Wiedersehen," the man said as he hurled Frank from the speeding train.

Chapter

13

FRANK REACHED OUT and latched on to the steel ladder, then ran to the roof of the train. His legs barely missed the ground rushing by in a blur. The sound of the wheels clacking over the tracks was deafening.

Frank looked down. His feet were about to get sucked under the train. Pulling with all his strength, he managed to get planted on the lowest step of the ladder.

Before he could get back inside the train, the thug appeared in the doorway and started kicking at his hands. Frank had to let go with his right hand; it felt as if his fingers were broken. His attacker kicked again, and this time Frank grabbed the booted foot and yanked. The man fell backward onto the floor of the car, and Frank quickly pulled himself in.

As the thug struggled to his feet, Frank threw two lightning-fast jabs. The black ski mask became wet with blood.

Then Frank saw a shadow loom over him. The second thug grabbed Frank by the hair and threw a hook at his ear. Spikes of pain blasted through his skull.

The door to the second-class cabin slid open, and Joe appeared. He grabbed the hood's arm before he could swing at Frank a second time. The man turned on Joe and snarled. Joe lunged forward, grabbed him in a choke hold, and rammed him against the wall of the car. His head left a spiderweb pattern in the glass.

A shrill whistle sounded as the conductor burst through the door separating the cars. Spitting the whistle from his mouth, he pulled Frank from the first masked thug. "What is this?" he demanded.

Immediately the second hood rushed toward the open outside door. As the conductor reached out to grab his arm, the crook leaped out into the night.

The conductor gasped.

Joe leaned out the doorway and looked up. He spotted the sole of a boot stepping off the top rung of the ladder.

The conductor crammed the whistle back in his mouth and blew it. Ignoring him, Joe reached for the ladder. The rungs were cold and icy, but he swung out anyway and clawed his way to the top.

Joe grasped the last rung and peered over the top. A boot came flying out of the darkness at his face. He ducked down and felt the shoe skim the top of his head. Then he heard a heavy thud.

The crook had slipped and fallen. Joe took his chance to scramble up the ladder. The guy rose to a crouch when he saw Joe. Without stopping to think, Joe put his hand on the back of the man's head and kneed him in the face. He screamed as he fell backward.

The train crossed an iron trestle, and the world began to rattle. Joe spread his arms to steady himself. Heedless of the danger, the fallen man pulled himself up to his feet and started to run. He hopped the space between the cars and headed for the front.

Joe took off after him, wondering where the guy was going. The train leaned to the left as it went around a curve. In the distance an over-hanging light turned from red to green. As the train moved forward, the railway signal became brighter until they were right under it.

The thug jumped for the light, hooking on to its supporting crossbar and swinging up like a world-class gymnast. Joe ducked as it passed overhead. He turned around and watched the figure get smaller as the train continued down the track.

"Unbelievable," Joe said to himself as he

headed back down the ladder. He descended one rung at a time, then carefully pulled himself back into the train.

"Are you okay?" Callie asked. Her face was pale and washed out in the bright lighting inside the car.

"He got away," Joe said. "What about your guy?"

"You won't believe it," Frank said, touching the scrape on the side of his head. "The guy took off into the next car. He must've jumped, because we couldn't find him anywhere."

"A couple of acrobats," Joe grumbled.

"Yeah, big ones." Frank flexed his fingers. They were bruised and cut but not broken.

They all sat down in the compartment. "That's not the first time we've seen two guys in black ski masks," Joe said, warming his hands under his armpits.

"You think they're working with Dr. Maxwell?" Callie asked.

"Dr. Maxwell had no idea we were going to the *Schneefest,*" Frank replied.

"Yeah, that's right." Joe leaned over to make sure the compartment door was locked. "Besides Stephi and Herr von Kubiza, only the guy who gave us the tickets knew we'd be here."

"Our good friend, Herr Gipfel," Frank said.

It was almost midnight when the Hardys and Callie completed the twenty-minute walk up from the train station. All the windows in the von Kubiza mansion were dark.

"Are we going to question Herr Gipfel tonight?" Callie asked.

"No," Frank said, remembering the net at Gipfel's front door. "I don't feel like running into a booby trap at this hour."

"We've got to do something." Joe rolled his shoulders, trying to relax. "There's no way I'm going to sleep tonight."

"Me, neither," Callie said.

"Well, we could stake out Gipfel's house," Frank suggested. "If those two thugs come back to report to him tonight, we'll have all the proof we need."

Callie held her finger up. "I'll take first shift."

They agreed that each person would take a two-hour shift, parking the van across the mountain road from Gipfel's house.

"If we see any action, we come back to the house and get the others, right?" Frank said.

"Right," Joe and Callie echoed.

After seeing Callie off for the first watch, Frank went up to his bedroom. He turned on his laptop and logged on to his online service. Then, leaving his computer on and still in his jeans and flannel shirt, he turned off the light and got in bed. He lay on his back, wide awake.

At 2:00 A.M. Callie knocked softly and stuck her head in the door.

"Nothing?" Frank asked.

"Not a peep."

"Okay, go get some sleep and I'll take the next shift."

Frank then spent two of the coldest, quietest hours of his life sitting in the van and staring at Gipfel's old, tilting house. He didn't see any activity.

He woke Joe at four in the morning and went back to his room. Frank felt as if he'd been asleep for less than five minutes when a persistent beeping noise nudged him awake. His travel alarm read 5:45 A.M. He'd been out for over an hour and a half.

The beeping continued. Frank rolled over and squinted at the lit screen of his computer. A tiny icon shaped like a letter flashed on and off, telling him he had new mail.

Frank clicked on the icon, and a letter from Vanessa scrolled onto the screen. "Ah, short but sweet," Frank said to himself.

Vanessa had written:

Joe, Frank, & Callie,
    Simulation done. Get your modem ready, and I'll transmit the data. Good luck.
                                        Vanessa

Joe opened the door without knocking. "Gipfel had no visitors last night."

"They're probably just lying low," Frank said. He turned the laptop around so Joe could read the message. "You ready to see what Vanessa came up with?"

Joe smiled. "Tell her we're tired of waiting."

They sat on the edge of the bed as Frank tapped away at the keyboard. A few minutes later faint outlines started to appear on the computer screen.

"It's like watching an invisible artist paint," Joe said. "Stuff just appears out of nowhere."

Frank pointed to a dark line at the top of the screen. "That's the Neckar River. She's sending us the Zimmermann property first."

Ten minutes passed. Finally the screen showed a detailed aerial photograph of Zimmermann's development.

"What good is this?" Joe said. "This is exactly the same as the photos I took from the plane."

"Just wait." Frank made sure all the data had been transmitted, then used the mouse to click on sections of the photograph. A vertical line swept across the screen and the photo changed.

"What'd you do?"

"I just removed a layer of soil," Frank said. He clicked the mouse again. Another layer of earth disappeared. "These lines are what we thought were the walls of the fort," Frank said, pointing out the dark, geometrical outlines. "Watch what happens to them."

As Frank removed more and more layers of soil, the dark outlines turned into one solid, filled-in surface the shape of a rectangle. After a few more clicks, the rectangle disappeared altogether, and only a couple of thin lines remained.

"See, now we're below the foundation of the house," Frank said. "Those lines are the water and sewer pipes that used to feed into it."

"That's amazing. So why did it look like the fort?"

"A foot or two of the original walls are still standing. That's what the photos picked up." Frank clicked the mouse twice, and the file closed. "Now for Gipfel's estate," he said.

This time the same long shadows they had seen before showed up.

"Those are the things Stephi said were sewer lines," Joe pointed out.

"Yup." Frank clicked off layers, and the shadows became a thick line, curving up to the top right-hand corner of the screen.

"Enlarge that part," Joe said.

Frank marked off a square section of the photo and clicked on it. Herr Gipfel's house came into view.

"See that?" Joe said. "This pipe thing doesn't even go close to the house. It goes right past it toward the cliff."

"That's not a sewer pipe," Frank said. "It's a stone trench, and a very old one." He enlarged another section and pointed to a tiny half-circle of darkness at the very top of the screen. "This is some sort of hole in the ground."

"Take off some layers. Let's see how deep it is."

Frank clicked the mouse several times. The dark spot didn't change. He clicked a few more times. Finally he reached the limits of Vanessa's simulation. The hole was still there.

"What in the world is that?" Joe asked.

Frank turned off the computer and folded down the screen. "There's only one way to find out."

Before they searched Gipfel's property, Joe insisted on going down into Herr von Kubiza's basement. Once there, he reached under the workbench for the crates of explosives.

"What are you planning to do with those?" Frank asked.

"I don't make plans, you know that." Joe carefully removed a couple of detonators and two of the smallest-shaped charges from the box. "Herr Gipfel likes booby traps, and I want to be ready for anything."

Joe put the detonators in one front pocket of his jeans and the coin-size explosives in the other.

Outside, there was a light dusting of snow on the ground, and the heavy clouds of the day before were breaking up to make way for the rising sun.

The brothers got in the van and drove the mile or so of winding road to Herr Gipfel's estate.

After they passed Gipfel's split-timbered house on their right, the road curved away from the cliff overlooking the river on the left. At this point there was a stretch of at least two hundred meters of rugged, rocky land between the road and the edge of the cliff. Frank pulled off the road and parked the van out of sight.

"If we read Vanessa's data right, that trench led up in this direction," Frank said. "If the fort is on Gipfel's land, it's between here and the cliff."

"I can't even see the cliff from here," Joe said. "The trees are too thick."

They started hiking through the stand of evergreens, ducking under brittle, dried limbs. The snow hadn't fallen long or hard enough to pass through the boughs of the trees, so the ground was a carpet of soft, clean-smelling pine needles.

Frank led the way until they came to a single strand of rusted barbed wire. It held a metal sign that read *Vorsicht Felsen.* Wind gusted up from the river, and the sign swayed back and forth. The breeze chilled the sweat on their faces.

Joe wiped his cheek with his jacket sleeve. "What's the sign say?"

"It says the cliffs are dangerous."

"No kidding." Joe ducked under the barbed wire and then held it up for Frank.

A few paces farther, the stand of trees ended and the earth dropped away into empty space.

Joe leaned over the cliff. It was a sheer drop of at least three hundred feet. "The river looks about as wide as a creek from up here," he said.

"Let's go upstream," Frank said.

The terrain close to the cliff was studded with rocks. As the Hardys climbed higher, the rocks grew larger. Joe stopped when he reached a tight crevice running between two huge boulders. "There's no way around," he said. "We'll have to work our way through here."

As he took a step up into the space between the rocks, Joe thought he saw something glint in the growing sunlight. He held his hand out, motioning for Frank to stop.

Bending down, Joe spotted a trip wire fashioned out of fishing line. It extended between the rocks at ankle height, then ran up to a slab of granite perched on top of the boulder nearest the cliff. "Another one of Gipfel's booby traps," Joe said.

Frank nodded grimly and stepped over the wire.

The passage narrowed until they had to turn sideways to squeeze through. After thirty feet or so, the left-hand wall began to fall away. Soon it disappeared completely, and they were on a two-foot-wide ledge. The wind picked up, carrying the smell of the river to them.

The ledge curved around the rock wall and brought them to a natural patio in the side of the cliff. A few startled birds launched themselves away and soared out over the river.

Joe noticed something strange. "Check this out, Frank." He started to walk over to a mound of fresh dirt. As he reached out to touch it, the ground gave way under his feet, and he felt himself plummeting through darkness.

Chapter

14

JOE INSTINCTIVELY BRACED HIMSELF for impact.
He hit hard and rolled to reduce the force, tum-
bling to a stop on a cold, stone floor. He lay still
for a second to make sure he wasn't hurt. Looking up, he saw a circle of blue sky about fifteen
to twenty feet above. Frank's face appeared in
the circle, blocking out the light that filtered in.

"Joe! Joe, are you okay?"

"I'm fine," Joe called, standing up. "I'm in
some sort of room or chamber." He found something like a ladder cut into the stone wall leading
up to the mouth of the hole. "I suggest you don't
take the express route, like I did," he added.

By the time Frank had climbed down the ladder, Joe's eyes had adjusted to the darkness.

"Look," he said, pointing to a doorway on the opposite wall of the chamber.

Frank spotted three Latin words carved into the stone above the door: *Castrum Caesaris Decii.* "Now we know what that dark spot on the computer screen was," Frank said.

"Yeah," Joe added. "A very clever hidden entrance to the fort."

"After you," Frank whispered, motioning toward the doorway.

Joe stepped through. The air was totally still, and a dry smell—like straw or old sawdust—hung in the corridor. The outside light reached only ten feet past the opening. Beyond that it was pitch black.

Frank snapped on his penlight. The walls and floor of the passage were coated with a fine dust of eroded rock. "It's like a tomb," he said. His words echoed back to him.

"Careful," Joe whispered. "Sound really carries down here."

As they moved into the carved-out mountain, the air became even more cold and dry, making it difficult to breathe.

Joe suddenly halted, putting a hand out to stop his brother. "Shhh," Joe said. "Listen." From deep inside the fort, they heard metallic clanking and distorted human voices. They continued on with even more caution.

About a hundred feet into the mountain, the passage ended at a T. From the right-hand corridor, Joe heard the ghostly echo of the voices. He pressed himself to the wall and peered around the corner. The hallway extended far into the darkness, but he could see a faint orange flicker of light coming from a door only a few yards down.

Together, the Hardys crept down the hall to the doorway, which opened to a small room filled with packing crates. A lit torch hung from a brace on the wall, sending its oily smoke up to the ceiling.

The room was unguarded, so Frank and Joe slipped inside. Frank pried the lid off one of the crates. The torchlight reflected off a dozen blades. "Swords," he said.

"The Roman arsenal." Joe lifted one of the weapons out of the box. He drew his thumb along the blade. Even after nearly two thousand years, it was still razor sharp. He passed it to his brother.

"Gipfel must be shipping them off to sell on the black market," Frank said.

Joe took a twelve-inch dagger for himself and slipped it into his belt. "Are you ready to get down to business?"

"Let's do it."

They left the room and continued down the corridor. Frank switched off his flashlight as the light in the passage became brighter. The sound of voices was more distinct now, and after a sudden turn to the left, the corridor opened up into a giant chamber.

"This must be the center of the whole complex," Joe whispered, crouching down behind the edge of the doorway. He could see from his hiding place that the huge chamber was round and, like the hub of a spoked wheel, had at least a dozen passages similar to theirs leading into it. More torches burned on the walls, and the air smelled of kerosene.

Frank crouched at the opposite side of the door, mouthing words silently to himself. When Joe glanced over, he pointed to a Latin inscription chiseled in giant letters on the vaulted stone ceiling. *"Ecce scutum Caesaris Decii. Reverete tuos hostes et cum reverentia tractaberis."*

"I can't make sense of it," Frank said.

The voices grew louder again, and Frank and Joe looked back into the chamber just in time to see three men emerge from one of the other corridors.

"Herr von Kubiza!" Joe hissed.

"And Karl and Johann," Frank added. "His two hired hit men."

The Hardys watched as Karl and Johann each dropped two heavy boxes onto a stack at the center of the chamber. The cook and the mechanic were covered with dirt and looked as if they hadn't slept for days.

Herr von Kubiza hammered his fist down on one of the wooden boxes. The sound rang through the chamber like a bass drum. He shouted something in German at the other two men. Karl and Johann nodded.

"He's asking them if they're sure they've searched the entire fort," Frank whispered.

"I cannot believe it!" von Kubiza stormed, this time in English.

An American voice came out of the shadows far across the chamber. "Yes, Egon. I told you it was a long shot."

"Shut up, Maxwell," von Kubiza shouted.

Frank and Joe exchanged shocked glances. Dr. Maxwell had also found the fort! It seemed their dad's friend *had* been involved all along. Was he in cahoots with von Kubiza and his goons?

Karl walked up to Herr von Kubiza and handed him a clipboard. "We have all the items ready for shipment," he said. "Once Maxwell finishes his work, we can finish loading and get out of here."

"What are you planning to do to me?" From the darkness, Dr. Maxwell's voice was hoarse and difficult to hear. And the man was clearly distressed. Maybe he wasn't in cahoots with von Kubiza after all.

Herr von Kubiza pulled one of the torches out of its wall bracket and carried it across the chamber. As the light shifted, Frank realized that four prison cells were carved into the far wall. And the first one had someone in it.

Dr. Maxwell pressed his face against the bars.

In the torchlight, he looked haggard and half-starved. "You promised you'd let me go," the archaeologist said.

Herr von Kubiza looked at him and began to laugh. "Well, my naive Dr. Maxwell, things have changed.

"You've got to let me out!" Dr. Maxwell cried, but von Kubiza had already turned away, leaving him in darkness.

Karl and Johann fell in behind von Kubiza as they crossed the chamber to the corridor leading back out to the cliffs—the very corridor that Frank and Joe were huddled in.

Frank knew they couldn't run for it; footsteps would attract attention. Instead, the Hardys pushed themselves deep into the stone corners. The torchlight angled through the doorway as Herr von Kubiza approached, barely leaving the two brothers in the shadows.

The three crooks passed within inches of Frank and Joe. The Hardys didn't relax until the footsteps faded away. Then they darted into the chamber.

"Frank and Joe Hardy!" Dr. Maxwell cried out. "How did you find me?"

Frank motioned for Maxwell to keep his voice down, then said, "It's a long story. Let's get you out of here first." He tugged at the cell door, but it was locked tight. "Shouldn't these bars be all rusted through?"

"Yes, yes. That's what's so remarkable about

this find," Dr. Maxwell said. "This fort has been sealed tight for almost two thousand years. Egon and his men had to do only a small amount of excavation at the entrance, and the air is so cold and dry down here that everything's been almost perfectly preserved."

"Here, let me give it a shot," Joe said, pulling his lock picks from his wallet. "Frank, grab a torch and hold it over here so I can see."

As Joe went to work on the lock, he asked Maxwell, "How did you get here?"

"I thought I saw a drainage trench on those measurements we took the day you got here," Dr. Maxwell said. "I went out with Egon to take some magnetic readings after dinner, and the data led us right to the edge of the cliff."

"But the entrance must have been hidden," Frank said, turning the torch so it would burn evenly.

"Yes, yes. We found a stone slab, and the readings told us there was a passage beneath it. When we pried the marker off, we were sure we'd finally discovered the lost fort."

"And then von Kubiza turned on you," Joe said.

"Yes, sadly," Dr. Maxwell replied. "He pulled a gun on me, took my keys, and locked me in this cell. The only reason I'm still alive is that he needed me to identify the artifacts so he'd know what he was selling on the black market."

"So Karl and Johann used your keys to break

into the carriage house and Zimmermann's lot," Joe said. Maxwell seemed surprised to hear this. "Von Kubiza wanted us to think you were trying to destroy your own research," Joe added.

"I'm sure you're right," Dr. Maxwell said. "There were rumors that he did the same thing on a dig in Turkey. He found the site, sold the artifacts, and reported to the authorities that he'd found nothing. If he convinces people that this fort never really existed, no one will ever be able to trace what he sells."

Joe struggled with the lock. "The mechanism is old and heavy. I can't get it to turn." He pulled the dagger from his belt and worked the tip into the lock.

Frank pointed to the ceiling. "This inscription says something about the shield, doesn't it?"

"Ah, yes," Dr. Maxwell said. He repeated the words aloud without looking up, reciting them in a weary tone. " '*Ecce scutum Caesaris Decii. Reverete tuos hostes et cum reverentia tractaberis.*' Those words haunted me every moment I was here. 'Behold the shield of Caesar Decius: respect your enemies and with respect you will be treated.' "

Maxwell looked at Frank, then Joe, and sighed. "I had enough time down here to figure it out." He pointed upward and said, "That's it. That's the shield."

"You mean there is no shield?" Frank asked.

"Exactly," Dr. Maxwell replied. "That piece of advice on the ceiling is Emperor Decius's shield."

"But what about the gold shield with rubies and emeralds? The one in the painting?" Joe almost had the bolt turned.

"Just a legend," Dr. Maxwell said. "I haven't told Egon yet. I knew he'd keep me alive only as long as he kept searching for it."

Joe looked up from the bolt and saw a sudden change in Maxwell's expression, which went from weary to alarmed. Swallowing hard, Joe realized that something was behind him—and that it wasn't a rescue party.

"It cost me half a million dollars to conduct that search," von Kubiza said, sneaking up behind Joe and Frank. Karl and Johann stood on either side of him. "But the rest of the armory is worth a small fortune." Joe turned around just in time to see von Kubiza pull a 9mm Sig Sauer pistol from his coat and level it at his head.

Chapter

15

KARL LIFTED A SET of keys from his belt and unlocked the cell door. Then Herr von Kubiza ushered Frank and Joe inside with a wave of his handgun. The iron door slammed behind them.

"You boys," von Kubiza said, resting his chubby hand on the crossbar. "You could not just enjoy my hospitality, could you? You had to pry where it was not your business to do so."

"Yeah, this is some kind of hospitality," Joe spat.

Herr von Kubiza twisted the end of his mustache. "I am sorry I cannot continue to be as good a host as I was. Now that I know there is no shield, it is time to finish up here."

"What about us?" Frank asked, though he already knew.

"Regrettably, there will be a cave-in later this morning," von Kubiza said. "No one will ever know there was a fort here, and the three of you will be buried alive."

Herr von Kubiza stepped back from the cell and nodded to Karl and Johann. "Keep watch on my guests while I fetch the explosives."

After von Kubiza disappeared, Frank began exploring the eight-by-ten cell. The ceiling was only about six feet high. He could barely stand up straight. Four sets of iron manacles hung from the walls. He tugged at the chains, but they were firmly attached.

When Dr. Maxwell spoke, he sounded as if he'd long since accepted his fate. "Believe me, I've searched the whole cell hundreds of times. There's no way out."

Joe shook his head. "I'm not so sure," he whispered. He waited for Karl and Johann to move farther away. When they seemed to be busy hammering the lids on the last few crates, Joe pulled the shaped charges and detonators from his pocket.

"Are you crazy?" Frank blurted.

"Shhh." Joe held the explosives close to his chest. "What other choice do we have?" Using his body as a shield to keep von Kubiza's men from seeing what he was doing, Joe carefully wedged one charge at the foot of the door and another at the lock.

He then unspooled the detonator wires and inserted them into the plastic explosive. When he touched the ends of the two wires together, the door would blow.

"Crouch down in the corner," Joe said. "No, wait." He looked at how he'd placed the charges.

"What's the matter?" Frank whispered.

"I don't like it," Joe said. He went back to the door and changed the angle of the charges slightly. "Now we'll find out if shaped charges really work the way they're supposed to."

The three of them huddled down in the far corner of the cell.

Joe heard Karl shout at them, "What are you doing in there? Stand up so we can see you!"

Joe heard the sound of footsteps coming to the door and, holding his breath, touched the wires together.

The explosion echoed through the chamber like a sonic boom. Frank felt the blast pressure slam him into the stone wall, and he thought he blacked out for a moment. When he stood up, he saw that the door had been torn completely off its hinges. It lay on the floor in a twisted heap.

Joe helped Dr. Maxwell to his feet. When the cloud of dust began to clear, they found Karl sprawled out on the floor, unconscious.

"This way!" Frank shouted.

Then Johann's hulking figure materialized

through the smoke. He rushed at Joe, wielding a heavy Roman broadsword.

Joe kept his eye on the sword. As Johann lunged at him, he stepped forward and to the right. The blade passed inches from his torso.

Joe leaned back and fired a crescent kick into Johann's midsection. Johann staggered back but didn't lose his grip on the sword. "Come on," Joe taunted. "Come after me."

Frank pushed Dr. Maxwell back and circled around von Kubiza's man.

Johann swung the blade in a wide arc. Joe ducked. He felt the blade sever the tips of his hair.

Frank rushed at Johann from behind, locking him in a choke hold. Joe moved in quickly. With a powerful, precise karate chop to Johann's thick wrist, the man was disarmed. The sword clattered to the floor.

Johann twisted and struggled, trying to throw Frank off his back, but Frank held on like a pit bull. Gradually the color drained from Johann's face as Frank pinched the carotid artery closed. Johann's thrashing grew weaker, and a few seconds later he was unconscious.

Frank let go, and the German slumped to the floor.

A long, low rumble, like distant thunder, rolled through the chamber. Then a thick cloud of dust spewed from the hallway leading to the cliff.

"What was that?" Dr. Maxwell asked.

"It's von Kubiza!" Frank shouted. "He's caving in the fort!"

"But his men are still here with us," Dr. Maxwell said.

"If he kills us all, there are no witnesses," Joe said. He reached down and wedged his hands under Johann's massive shoulders. "Help me, Frank."

With his brother's help, Joe lifted Johann to a sitting position. He then squatted down and heaved with all his strength. The going got a little easier once he had the big man slung over his shoulder. "Can you get Karl?" he asked. But Frank was already coming back across the chamber, carrying Karl's limp body like a seasoned fireman.

Another explosion shook the fort. With Dr. Maxwell leading the way, they stumbled down the corridor in the direction of the exit. Dust and shards of rock rained down on them. The force of the next explosion blew out the torches, throwing them into almost total darkness.

"Follow me!" Dr. Maxwell shouted over the noise.

But Joe could barely see Dr. Maxwell in front of him. When Johann started to slip from his shoulder, Joe had to stop and lift him again. He called for Frank behind him.

"I'm here!" Frank shouted. "Don't slow down for me."

The explosions seemed to come from right

above them now. Joe fell to one knee. A hand reached out of the darkness for him, pulling him to his feet.

Joe looked up and there it was, blue sky above them. He followed Dr. Maxwell up the ladder to the fresh air outside.

When he made it to the top, he dumped Johann and turned back. He didn't see Frank. The next explosion caused earth and dead leaves to fall into the fort entrance. Joe dropped to his knees and looked in. Frank was only halfway up the ladder.

Frank's head was covered with dirt. The hole started to cave in around him, and he reached up in desperation. He found his brother's hand and gripped it with all his strength. With Karl still over his back, he took another step up the ladder. Joe hoisted him up, and Frank emerged from the hole, on top of Karl. Frank rolled onto his back and watched the fort entrance collapse into a sinkhole of loose earth and rocks.

At that moment Herr von Kubiza approached from the ledge. He froze in surprise.

"Come back to check on your handiwork?" Frank asked. He stood up to face von Kubiza.

The German turned to run back the way he'd come, but Joe cut him off. Von Kubiza went for his gun, but this time Joe was ready. With a snapping front kick, he knocked the pistol from von Kubiza's hand. It sailed out over the cliff.

Herr von Kubiza raised his hands in the air in a gesture of surrender.

"I figured you didn't have the guts to fight it out without your two thugs," Joe said.

The next morning Frank, Joe, and Callie loaded their bags into the Porsche. Callie was still a little bit mad at Frank for not waking her up to search for the fort, but he knew her spirits would pick up as soon as they hit the slopes. The teenagers planned to take the last few days of winter break to do some skiing in the German Alps.

"Oh, man," Joe complained as he lifted his duffel into the car. "I'm still sore from carrying Johann."

"I could use a good night's sleep," Frank added. They'd been up half the night explaining everything to the police, while Stephi tried to help Gabi cope with her father's arrest.

Stephi and Dr. Maxwell walked out of the carriage house and up to the three. "I don't know how I'll ever be able to thank you enough," Dr. Maxwell said, shaking hands with the Hardys. "I hope your father isn't upset with me for getting you mixed up in such a dangerous situation."

Joe smiled. "Don't worry, Dr. Maxwell. He knows we would have gotten into some sort of danger without your help, anyhow."

Dr. Maxwell laughed and clapped Frank on the shoulder. "And I hope you will both consider a career in archaeology. You have quite a talent for it."

"Thanks," Frank said. "But I think I'll leave that to Stephi." He held the passenger door open, waiting for Callie to get in.

Stephi gave her a hug. "I got this for you," she said, pulling a compact disk from her purse. "It's by that band you saw at the snow party, *Tote Gebäde.*"

"Awesome!" Callie kissed Stephi on the cheek and wished her luck. Then she got in the car and they were ready to go.

Joe put the Porsche in gear and headed down the driveway. At the turn onto the mountain road, Frank stopped him, putting his hand over the shift knob.

"Hold on a second," Frank said. "That's Herr Gipfel coming."

Frank rolled down his window, and Herr Gipfel stuck his head inside. "I was afraid you would leave before I saw you," he said, resting his metal hand on the roof of the car.

"I guess since the artifacts were on your property, you just became a millionaire," Callie said.

Herr Gipfel shook his head. "I am a very simple man. I have my apple orchard, my old house. Who needs more? I've decided to donate all the artifacts to the government, along with enough land to build a museum. I only regret that most of the fort was destroyed."

"Here," Frank said. "I forgot to give you this."

He reached into his pocket, found the gold Roman coin, and held it out to Gipfel.

"No, you keep that," Herr Gipfel said. He smiled as Joe shifted into first. "Just don't let German customs find it. They'll never let you out of the country."

Frank and Joe's next case:

Frank and Joe have come to the ruggedly beautiful mountains of Utah to test their wilderness skills. But on their very first day out, after a frayed rope nearly sends Joe plummeting to the bottom of a rocky ravine, they discover that the challenge will be far more perilous than they imagined. This will be a test of survival! The Hardys have stumbled upon a deadly scheme of greed and sabotage. But to discover the secret behind it, they'll have to follow the trail of infamous outlaws—Butch Cassidy and his Hole in the Wall gang. The gang may be long gone, but a new breed of desperado is on the loose, and they're gunning for Frank and Joe . . . in *Survival of the Fittest,* Case #120 in The Hardy Boys Casefiles™.